A GANGSTA GIRL AND HER BULLY

BY ROBIN & KASHA

This is a work of fiction. All of the characters, organizations, and events portrayed in this novel are either a product of the author's imagination or are used fictitiously. Any resemblance to actual persons, living or dead, is purely coincidental.

PROLOGUE

How it all started....

"Fuck!"

"Fuck!"

"Fuck!"

Kane shouted as he banged his hand on the island in his kitchen. He was still holding his Obama phone in his hand. He banged his hand so hard, his phone broke into pieces.

"Fuck!" he shouted again, this time, grabbing his four-year-old daughter's attention.

"Daddy, are you okay? Why did you break your phone?" Kayley asked in the sweetest tone. Kane knew he had to calm his temper in front of his little girl.

Kane was a hardcore gangster from South Carolina, but when it came to his daughter, he put all his devilish ways to the side. He bent down on one knee and caressed his daughter's face. He smiled.

"It wasn't working, so I had to open it, baby," he lied.

He couldn't tell his daughter that his trap house had gotten shot up, and somebody was a rat on his team. Kayley lived a sheltered life. She had never been to a crack house and the only coke she knew was Coca-Cola.

"Daddy, you cursed too. Why did you say that bad word? Now, you have to put money in the swear jar," she pointed her tiny finger that the cookie jar on the counter that read: *swear jar.*

At that moment, Kane heard the front door open and heels clicking on his wooden floors.

"Key, go upstairs and go to bed, I'll be up in a minute," Kane said before his wife, Bossee, came into the kitchen.

"But I want to stay up with mommy," Keyley whined.

"She'll be up later, now go," Kane said in a firm tone.

Keyley knew when her dad was serious, so she marched her little butt right to her room and closed the door.

“Kane, I’m here where are you, baby, I’m sorry I’m late, I had—”

Before Bossee could get another word in, Kane had her hemmed up on the wall, aggressively, tugging on her North Face jacket. It was nine in the evening, and it was at least thirty degrees outside. They lived in South Carolina where it was always cold.

“So, you just walk into my fucking house the next day and think it’s all cool? Where the fuck you been? The nanny left an hour ago,” Kane said in a low yet aggressive tone.

“Don’t fucking grab me, nigga. I told you, I danced last night, and I was going to a pole class today. I stayed at Lexy’s last night so I wouldn’t have to drive all the way home in the rain. I just left the class an hour ago. I thought you would at least want to spend time with your daughter while the nanny was gone," Bossee yanked away from Kane and walked over to the refrigerator.

"Yeah, you better be just fucking dancing Bossee. I don't know why you still want to be a stripper and you have a child at home and a nigga with money."

Bossee hated when Kane brought up the fact that she wasn't always home with Keyley. She loved her daughter, but she loved dancing too. It wasn't about the money, at times. But she loved feeling sexy in the club and dancing. It was somewhat a hobby to her. She took her time with her dances. She didn't drink and she didn't smoke while she was at the strip club. Also, Kane made her sign a contract that she wouldn't smoke or drink at work. She also didn't cheat on Kane like he thought. Since she hung around a bunch of rowdy females, Kane and his homies, thought birds flock together.

However, Kane, on the other hand, hated the fact that she wanted to dance. All he saw in the strip club were whores and gold diggers. He knew most of the women in the strip club had one goal and that was to make some money. Most of them had no limits to what they would do, and he often heard in the streets that his wife was no better than the next bitch in the club. He wanted to believe his wife was faithful, but sometimes, he didn't know about her. But she didn't know about him either because he was a known cheater.

"Don't come at me like that Kane. I just came home and I'm tired!" Bossee shouted back at him with an attitude. She was tired, and she knew she had to be up with Keyley for the rest of the night.

"Well, my trap house got shot up and I have to find out what happened. You told me you would be home at seven and it's nine. I hope your ass staying home for the rest of the week. Keyley got some curricular activities all week and she need her mama," Kane swept his keys off the counter and headed to the door.

"You're always thinking I'm the whore, and you're always in the streets, fuck you, Kane!" Bossee shouted.

The only thing Bossee heard was her front door slam. She loved Kane but she knew they were going down the wrong path. They married too young and their lives were moving too fast. But she promised she would never leave her husband. She continued to pray that her and Kane fell back in love with each other like they did years ago. Although Kane was a drug dealer, and it was just as a bad sin as what she was doing, she had always known it.

She knew that was all he knew, and she respected it. Kane was the reason they lived the way they lived in the suburbs. He paid for the house, the cars, and everything Keyley and Bossee owned. He never asked her for cash. She was able to keep all her tips and she was making just as much as he was.

Bossee took her mind off Kane. She reached in the refrigerator and pulled out some chocolate ice cream. She had a movie from Redbox and she was going to watch it over a bowl of ice cream with her daughter.

CHAPTER ONE

That same night…

Kane bundled up in his faux fur coat as he made his way to the front door of his apartment, also known as his dope spot. It was unbelievable that his spot had gotten shot up and no one called the police. Everyone in the neighborhood didn't mess with Kane or his spot. They knew anything that went down at his spot, the police wouldn't handle. Nobody wanted Kane to get knocked either.

He walked into his dope spot and immediately became angry when a cloud of cigarette smoke slapped him in the face.

"Yo, what the fuck you niggas been doing all day? The windows are fucking shot out and you niggas in here having a party? Pick these fuckin pizza boxes up. You niggas are scums, man," Kane said as he tossed an old pizza box to the floor.

"Where the fuck is that nigga Mikey at?" he asked.

No sooner than he said that, Mikey came walking from the back.

Mikey was Kane's right-hand man. They had been friends since they were kids. His mother and Kane's mother were best friends and raised them together. Mikey was the opposite of Kane. Kane was tall with caramel skin with a fade like Nas. Mikey was dark skin with long dreads that fell down his back. The ladies loved his long dreads. He had been growing them since a teen. However, he was sloppy, and Kane was sick of it. He left him in charge of his operation, and something was happening every week.

"Bro, them niggas from downtown Charleston came and shot our shit up. Word on the street is them niggas did that because of that party we attended last weekend," Mike flopped down on the couch and snatched the blunt from one of their little soldiers.

Kane thought about it.

"This shit is petty, bro. We getting shot at for being fly?" Kane expressed.

He was stressed out, and tired of dealing with niggas in the street. He was ready to go low-key and start a new venture, and it didn't require careless niggas.

"I told you we need to be low-key while we on this drug shit heavy. Now we gotta pack up the spot and relocate," Mikey expressed and handed the blunt to Kane.

"Nah, niggas need to know we are not to be fucked with. Load y'all shit up, we finna go find these niggas," Kane said as he walked to the back of the house with Mikey in tow.

That night bloodshed was like no other. Kane showed no love to his enemies and wanted to send a message that he was not to be played with.

CHAPTER TWO

The following day

"Girl, you know you and Kane love each other, and you know he's right. You don't need to be dancing, you need to be at home with Keyley," Bossee's best friend said through the phone.

"Girl I know, but it's boring being a house bitch all day here in South Carolina, I can at least go out and do my thing at night."

"I guess girl. You know me, I wish I didn't have to dance. I wish I found me a drug dealer nigga. I'd be trying to team up."

"Yeah, I hear you. Well let me go in this house and start dinner. I have Keyley in the backseat. We just sitting in the garage. This wind is blowing out of control."

"Okay girl talk to you later."

Bossee got out her passenger and took her daughter from the back seat. They walked through the house through the garage and Keyley shot straight to her room. Bossee went back outside and got her groceries and items from Target. She had spent the day shopping for the house and taking Keyley to her swimming and gymnastics classes. It was still raining, and word was they could possibly be flooded in, so she racked up on everything she was going to need for the week.

"Sick of all this rain, I wish we could move to Cali," Bossee fussed as she closed her garage door and got slapped in the face with hail. She hated rain and ice.

She didn't know how she survived for so long in South Carolina. Bossee walked back into her house and went to her room. She changed into some cleaning clothes and got to it. Bossee and Kane shared a huge five-bedroom house and Bossee cleaned every room and bathroom while sipping wine with her headphones in. She was feeling herself as she danced and sang around the house. She made her way and started prepping her dinner.

Once dinner was on, she took off her head buds and flopped on the couch. She sat silent with her eyes closed and remembered Kane had been home all day locked in his man cave. He crept in about three in the morning and locked himself in his space. Bossee figured he was still mad since he didn't sleep in bed with her so she gave him space all day. But she knew it was time to break the ice.

Bossee walked up the stairs and headed to the back of the house. She knocked softly on the door, and then heard Kane tell her to come in. When she walked in, the room was dim. The huge flat screen he had mounted on the wall was on, but he had it on mute. Kane was sitting on the couch with a notebook and pen in his hand. He looked up and gave her a half smile, and Bossee gave him the same smile back. As she was about to sit next to him, she glanced at the paper he was writing on.

The top said *Bitch Gang,* and then at the bottom of *Bitch Gang,* it said *Bossee Bitch.* Bossee sat down next to him.

"What's up, daddy, what you doing?" she asked, even though she already knew what he was doing.

"Jotting down a few of my thoughts," he said nonchalantly as he traced over the things he had already written.

"Well I know you been pissed off at me, so I want to apologize. I did some thinking overnight, and I decided to not dance anymore," Bossee admitted.

She only decided to quit dancing because she knew what Kane was mapping out on his notepad. He had been talking about it for the last year, and she realized he was ready to put his plan in action.

"It's all good, and I apologize too. I know you not a hoe, but you dancing in S.C clubs make you look like one. I see your vision, and you got this hustle shit from me. I know you staying at home twenty-four seven being a soccer mom is not realistic, so I'm finally ready to form my girl gang, and I got a plan that includes you."

She shifted her weight to one side and raised her eyebrow.

"Includes me?"

"First off let me say, I know you are tired of living in my hometown in this weird weather, so I'm moving us to Cali so you are close to your family, and Keyley has all the babysitters you will need."

Bossee beamed at his words. She left California with Kane seven years prior. He was there on business and Bossee was on the arm of his plug named Flex. It was like love at first sight for them. Kane just had to have Bossee, and little to his knowledge, Bossee knew she had to have him too. Three days later, her ex came up missing, and within a month, his body showed up in pieces. That's when Kane made his move, and Bossee didn't think twice when Kane asked her to be his wife.

That's when she fled to S.C when it was confirmed to be her Flex's body getting sent to her home. Come to find out when Kane found out the way Flex was treating her and witnessed him slapping Bossee across the face in front of everyone, he had to step in. He had gotten Flex kidnapped and Kane handled him himself. Bossee had been with him ever since and thanked him every day for saving her. Kane had never put his hands on her and kept his promise to always be faithful. So, she couldn't have asked for more.

"Thank you, Kane. I'm so ready to go back home. I've been calling my mother everyday but she always tells me I'm okay here. And I am okay here. But I would love to be back home."

"We can start packing up the house and putting it up for sale in a month."
Bossee was excited.

"Okay, so what's the plan with this girl gang? I'm curious."

"I got two hundred kilos buried at the bottom of our house. Nobody knows this but you. But I can't get it off in S.C, so we gotta get out of here and expand. Niggas is shooting up my spot and they know where I keep my work. I'm cool on fucking with niggas. So, I need you to build me a team of solid females from South Carolina to California. Loyal bad bitches only, Bossee, and you gotta make them all *my* bitches," Kane stroked his chin.

"Damn, Kane, that was a mouth full, but you know I got you baby. But what's with me making them your bitch? You trying to pimp?"

Kane chuckled. "Nah, rename them all, your name is *Bossee Bitch* when you ain't around Keyley. You smart, you know what I mean."

She smiled, "Daddy is a genus, I love that," she said as she climbed onto his lap.

Bossee was pleased about his plan, now she was ready to celebrate.

CHAPTER THREE

After Kane got the same construction workers that buried his dope under the house, he got them to dig it right back up. He was on a mission, a mission that was going to set him and Bossee up to be rich forever. He already had dough, but the shit he was sitting on was going to bring them millions, but there was no way he could get it all in one batch. So, he had a list of drug dealers from coast to coast, and his new crew was going to deliver it. However, he had to wait for Bossee to build the team.

"Damn, you had that shit tucked, for real," Bossee walked up and said to him, snapping him out his thoughts.

"This was the only way I knew the Feds wouldn't get it. Let's walk to the garage and talk some business," Kane said as it started to drizzle.
The two walked into the garage.

"So, this is the list of some of the stuff I want done when we get to Cali. You can start looking for girls soon as we get settled in. After you set it up, I want you to set up a meeting with everyone. If we keep this going for a year, we will be almost millionaires. So, let's keep it simple for now when we move. I promise in a year, money will never be an issue, not that it is now." Kane slid her the list and she gazed at it.

"I'm already steps ahead of you. I have five girls lined up in Cali that I trust, and they with whatever I got going on. You just sit back and watch me make it happen. I won't let you down."

Bossee kissed Kane on the lips and walked in the house. Kane walked back over to the construction workers feeling good. He knew his plan was going to work, but he had no idea how great yet deadly it was going to turn out…

THE START OF THE BITCH GANG...

Bossee and Kane settled in their new home with Keyley three months after they had left S.C. The entire time Bossee made sure she met with the girls individually to see exactly what was up with them. Being gone for seven years, she wanted to ensure she picked the crew, delicately. Kane would never let her live it down if she fucked up, so she did background checks on them.

Everyone was clean and their hood report came back great, and today was the day they would meet Kane. She didn't really give them too many details as to the what they would be doing as of yet, in case things didn't check out with their records. Over the years Kane had instilled in her the art of moving undetected, so she rented a suite at the Aloft for the meeting.

She hired a personal chef to prepare dinner, and had gotten them each a *Bitch* necklace, should they accept their offer. She put the packet containing their contract inside her Gucci book bag and went downstairs to meet Kane in the car. Keyley was at her mother's house for the weekend so she had nothing to worry about, except getting to the money.

"Damn, sexy lady! I almost wanted to take you back in the house and crush them guts," Kane said as he licked his plumped lips.

Reaching over her, he gave his wife a wet kiss, then proceeded to their destination. It was an hour drive to Malibu from their home in Beverly Hills, and they plan to spend the weekend at the suite. Traffic was light being that it was early in the morning, so the drive seemed really quick. When they arrived, Kane had the bellboy gather their belongings while they checked into their room. Once inside Bossee began to prepare for the girls arrival. Moments later the chef arrived with the requested menu for the night, already prepared.

Bossee let him setup the massive lunch that consisted of crab cake sliders, maple bread with soft cheese, roasted chicken with Balsamic Sauce, Orzo Salad, and Cheese and Spinach Puff Pastry Pockets. She decided to select an array of things so that everyone would have something to enjoy. After placing a packet next to each person's designated seat, she made her way to the lobby to greet the women due to arrive within the next ten minutes.

The first to arrive were her twin cousins, Torrica and Trendini, in a canary yellow Bentley GT sport. The twins were her first cousins, Bossee's mother and their mother were twins also, so they grew up really close. People actually thought that they were all sister growing up because of how they favored each other. Torrica, was the finesse queen in Cali. She made all the ballers kick out money when they were under her spell. The sisters striking beauty made their targets fall for them on sight. Both sisters were wearing colorful long lace fronts.

Torrica's hair was yellow like the car, and Trendini's was mint green. They were both very light skin, tall, and slim thick. They knew they were popping with their slanted grey eyes, and pouty pink lips. Trendini was known for her obsession to flashy things, hence the dope ride they pulled up in. She always had to have the new, new of everything. She was great at stealing whatever her heart desired. That's why Bossee gave them the names *Finesse Bitch* (Torrica) and *Flashy Bitch* (Trendini).

The second to arrive, seconds later was Nezzy in a snow-white Ferrari. She and Bossee met through Bossee's ex, Flex. She was mixed with Black and Mexican, and gorgeous in a plastic barbie kind of way. She paid thousands of dollars for her perfect body, and structured face. She used to run packages for Flex, and she and Bossee became super tight. Flex fired Nezzy after she worked for about two years for him because she didn't take shit from anyone and she was a certified goon. She wouldn't backdown when he tried to punk her and treat her like shit. She was bat shit crazy when she was mad, and didn't mind fucking up some shit.

She was real smart with computers and the queen of hacking shit so, Bossee named her *Gangsta Bitch.* The twins, Nezzy, and Bossee greeted each other and made small talk as Equadree and Askaria pulled up together in an old school tricked out 69 Cutlass. Equadree had been Bossee's friend since middle school. She doesn't have a beautiful body but she's cute in the face. She kept her hair in a low fade, and her waves was on swim. She was a pretty stud and was known in the hood for shooting a nigga or bitch. She'd been trapping for years and could sell just about anything. She ran six blocks in Cali, at the moment, so it was only right that Bossee named her *Trap Bitch.*

Askaria was Equadree's girlfriend of four years. She was young, only twenty-five. She was thicker than a snicker, with rich dark skin, she was a real beauty. She had long blonde bundles that complimented her warm skin tone. Her loyalty was to E, who was the love of her young life. On any given day you could catch her bagging up and serving right beside E. After a rough upbringing, she was finally living a good life. Bossee named her *Young Bitch.*

Bossee led the ladies to the suite where Kane was patiently waiting to start their meeting. When the ladies walked in, Kane greeted them each with a handshake.

"Ladies, welcome and thank you for giving us time out of your life. Every person has an assigned seat, please find your names on the placement cards," Kane started as he gestured for the ladies to have a seat.

"Are those crab cake sliders? Yes! I haven't had those since we were little girls B!" Torrica yelped excitedly as she found her chair and grabbed a plate. Clearing his throat Kane made his way to his seat and started the meeting.

"I'm sure you're wondering exactly why we brought you girls together today, so I'm about to just jump right in. You all have folders, if you open them, the first page has the amount I'm willing to pay you upfront should you accept a position with us. Every one of you have a certain skill that would make a shit ton of money."

"Two hunnit bands!! I'm in, I don't care what fuck we doing," Nezzy interrupted Kane when she opened her folder and saw the offer.

"Glad, you feel that way Nezzy. From my understanding you're the person I need to handle transportation. As stated in the contract, you will need to find a safe route from coast to coast. It's a really big job though. Can you handle it?" Kane asked with a smirk.

"They call me point A, Point B where I'm from. I can do that in my sleep!" Nezzy said with confidence.

Bossee smiled and gave Nezzy a head nod because she knew that she was stating facts. During the duration of the meeting Kane ran down each task the girls would be required to do should they accept and sign the contract. Torrica was in charge of getting the scoop on every heavy hitter in the state, so Kane could find a way to take over their blocks. Trendini was in charge of getting and taking them down by setting them up and robbing them, before Kane killed them. Equadree was in charge of setting up and running the traps that Kane would open, starting in three weeks.

Askaria would be in charge of distributing the product to each trap, and second counting the money. Bossee would be in charge of the girls, and also in charge of finding new clientele for the business. After running everything down so that everyone understood their position, Kane was happy to see every *BITCH* had signed and agreed. They also understood that they were all required to sell as much cocaine they could in bulk. *I'll be billionaire within the next two years,* he thought as he kissed Bossee on the lips as they all raised their glasses to celebrate.

CHAPTER FOUR

A week later…

Trendini switched her ass as she made her way through *Club Perdro's.* It was a Mexican club and she stood out like a sore thumb, but she didn't care one bit. She made sure her breast were pushed up to her chin in the bralette she wore for this job tonight. As she walked, she ignored all the hoots and cat calls. Instead, she scanned the area she knew her target, Smoke, would be. Making her way over, she stood in front of him boldly with a sexy smile.

Smoke had three bitches all over him but Trendini had his attention immediately. Dismissing the women with a flick of his wrist by shooing them away, he gave Trendini his full attention.

"Hey, Big Daddy. I'm the new cowgirl around these parts, I've come to show you just that," Trendini whispered to him as he leaned over to his ear. Confusion lines along with the other wrinkles made his face appear angry, but he really wanted to know what this beautiful lady meant. Not wanting him to wait for an answer any longer, Trendini sat on his lap comfortably licking her plump lips.

"I want to be your wife, and with a pussy as clean as this, I'm sure I can do that."

She continued rubbing her ass on his stiff package she felt rising. Trendini made sure to stare him in his eyes as she rocked back and forth on his dick. *Bingo!* she thought when he invited her to his estate a couple songs later.

Smoke was the Migo plug in Cali. He supplied over half of the state. Bossee and Kane decided three days ago that this is who they needed to take down first. *Kill the head, the body follows!* Kane explained in their brief meeting. Trendini knew this wasn't going to be an easy mark, and was fully prepared to wrap him up, even if she had to become his wife. She needed to make sure that before she killed him, she knew where everything was. Kane was planning to take over the entire state, too bad

Smoke turned down a chance to do business with the *Bitch Gang.* It was going to not only cost him his business, but also his life.

Smoke and Trendini made their way out the back to his awaiting car. They both slid into the back seat of his charcoal grey Phantom. Immediately they began heavy kissing, licking, and feeling over each other. Trendini got on her knees in front of Smoke and pulled her long mint green bundles in a messy bun on top her head. She unzipped his pants and devoured his tiny five-inch dick as if it was the best thing since slice bread. She also gagged with all the hair that surrounded his dick and balls, but she pushed it out her head.

She made loud sucking sounds as she popped her jaws dramatically and twisted her tongue around his dick. Moments later her was cumming and screaming in Spanish.

“Sucking dick like that will have you being wifey in no time,” Smoke expressed as he flipped Trendini over to snatch her panties off.

Damn, I hope I can nut off this little ass dick, she thought as she discreetly rolled her eyes. Trendini applied more glitter gloss on her lips and paid attention to her surroundings.

"I'm not finished with you Mamí, when we get home I'm going to work that beautiful body," Smoke spoke with broken English.

"I'm *dying* to get there, baby," Trendini replied with pun intended, because someone was sure to die tonight.

Smoke excitedly rubbed his hands over his penis with lust in his eyes. He couldn't believe that this *nigga of a woman* was in love with him already. Smoke planned to fuck her in every hole of hers and let her choke on his dick all night. He was sure that after he did her body right, she would marry him, and he would be legally in the States. What he didn't know was Trendini had her own plans for him.

Twenty minutes later they pulled up to his home, Trendini wasn't impressed with the home because she'd seen bigger, but it would have to do.

She made mental notes as they entered and after the tour Smoke gave her, she was convinced she'd hit the jackpot. This was his stash house, she could tell by the armed guards surrounding the basement door that carried heavy artillery. Trendini secretly came in her panties at the thought of licking Smoke and completing her first task given by Kane. Reaching over into her Chanel purse she fished her iPhone out to send Bossee a text to put their men into place.

"Smoke, baby I need to freshen up for you daddy," Trendini cooed making sure to blink her lashes at him. She remembered passing a restroom near the basement during the tour, so she made her way towards it.

"This motherfucker isn't going to know what hit him," she exclaimed making her way inside the lavish restroom.

Checking her phone, she saw that Bossee had texted back to let her know everyone was in place. She gave her the green light to setup. Pulling the small bomb from her bag she placed it on the opposite wall away from the attached wall to the basement. Making sure it was in place and ready to go she made her way into the living area with Smoke.

"Smoke, I think I left my phone in the car," she lied to Smoke as she bit her lip and softly tapped her head in a forgetful manner. He offered to go with her but she ensured him that she was fine and stated that she needed to smoke a cigarette. After not much more rebutting he agreed so Trendini switched dramatically towards the front door.

When she saw the black Sprinter van, she hit the button on the detonator and listened out to Smoke and his soldiers scramble to make their way towards to front door. One by one Kane and his crew shot them down like an army, poor Smoke never saw his end coming.

"Job well done, cuzzo," Bossee said as Trendini made way inside of the decked-out van. Everyone was in attendance and rooted her on as she playfully took a bow. Part of phase one was now completed and they all were excited. Taking Smoke out would help them execute the rest of their plan because he was considered the top dog. Kane made his way inside of the van. He was all smiles and so were the girls. Seeing how happy he was made Bossee happy, so she reached over a peaked his lips.

"Let's take over this shit baby," he hollered making them all erupt into a fit of laughter.

CHAPTER FIVE

Two months later...

Bossee was sitting on her couch in her den, looking through Kane's phone while he showered and got ready for their meeting with the twins. She was furious as she looked through his phone at all the females that he was trying to connect with. They had only been in California five months and he was already slutting around. She thought he had left his dog ways in South Carolina, but clearly he didn't. She hated his slimy ways, but she loved him to the core. He did everything for her, and when they were good, they were good.

He had taken her from a fucked-up situation and she thanked him for that. But now, she was starting to feel like he was taking her kindness as weakness. That was one of her main reasons why she wanted to move back to California so she could shake his ass when shit got bad. She wasn't going to leave him and be stuck in S.C, so she figured she'd come to Cali, get the money, and then expose his ass.

"Remember why you here, Bossee," she said to herself as she closed his phone and tossed it back on the loveseat where she found it.

"Mommy, can I go play in my room now?" her daughter asked, snapping her out her thoughts.

"Yes, go ahead, your Nana will be here in a minute to watch you, and cook."

Her daughter ran off to her room and Bossee headed in the kitchen for something strong to drink. She had to get her mind right before the twins came and Kane came downstairs. She wasn't in the mood to blow his spot and the meeting they had with the twins was big. Besides Kane's infidelities, business was going really good. The girls were in place and were working the streets like pros.

Bossee pulled a bottle of wine from the fridge and then pulled out a large wine glass. She filled it up halfway and then added a shot of D'usse with a few pieces of ice. She stood there sipping her strong concoction in deep thought. So many times, she thought about leaving Kane and finding somebody that would appreciate her. She also knew she had enough money put up to be on her own. But she knew as long as Kane was living, she wasn't going anywhere. The thoughts made her so upset.

This nigga does not control me, she thought.

"What's up, babe? You good?" Kane asked when he stepped in the kitchen knocking Bossee out her thoughts.

"Yeah, I'm good why you asked that?" Bossee asked in a defensive tone, not realizing she had much attitude in her voice.

"Because you look like somebody pissed you the fuck off. You think I don't know that look?" he raised his eyebrow.

"I know you know this look, and you also should know I'm not no stupid ass bitch. But we're going to leave it at that."

Bossee walked off because their doorbell was ringing. She looked at her Rolex and it was five in the evening. The twins were just in time and she was glad because she was trying to get out of Kane's presence a.s.a.p.

"Bossee, wait up, what the fuck is up?" Kane asked with a confused look on his face.

"It's all good, Kane. Don't trip. I got my period this morning and I'm not in the mood. Let's get this business done, I'm going out with my cousin and I don't want to be late."

Kane shrugged his shoulders, "I'll be in my office waiting on y'all." He walked off shaking his head.

When Bossee opened the door, the twins stood there dressed in all black and their long black wigs were pulled into high ponytails. Honestly, she had known these girls her whole life, and still couldn't tell them apart. She called them twin and they both answered so it worked for her. They both had a duffle bag in each hand that looked heavy.

Bossee stepped to the side so that they could walk in. As soon as they stepped in the foyer, they dropped the bags to the floor.

"Damn, that shit looks heavy, must have been a helluva lick," Bossee said as he shut the door and locked it.

"Man, was it. Had to body a nigga and stuff em in a lil ass bag, that's definitely a helluva lick," Torrica said.

"It's bodies in there, bitch?" Bossee asked. "Take that shit to the backyard." She pointed towards the kitchen that led to the backyard.

"Kane told us to bring the nigga to him in pieces, I hope he got our fifty-grand too," Trendini replied.

The girls started dragging two of the duffle bags outside.

"The other two are money and coke," one of the twins said.

A trail of blood was left on Bossee's marble floors and she was pissed about it. She grabbed the remaining two bags and went up to Kane's office before the girls. When she walked in, Kane was putting money through his money machine. She dropped the bag on the floor and walked over to his desk.

"Here, babe, I wanted to give you your cut before the girls came up here," Kane said handing her a stack of money. She took it and sat in front of his desk.

"Thank you, but we have a problem. You told them bitches to bring a dead body to my house?" She gritted at him with a look of anger on her face.

"My bad, baby, I'll make sure that shit don't happen again. The nigga didn't want to get down with us or cut us a deal, so he had to go, you know the rules."

"I know rules are rules, but we got our lil mama in the house, we gotta respect her. It's blood all on my floors, Kane."

Kane nodded his head. "You're right, Bossee, I wasn't thinking. But damn, I just said it wouldn't happen again!" Kane spoke raising his voice.

Lately, his wife had been down his throat about even the smallest shit, and it was starting to work his nerves. In his eyes, he had upgraded Bossee's life all the way, so she should cut him some slack.

"I was going to tell you once I got the keys, but I rented out a house for the girls to do business out of. It's nice too, up in the hills away from the public. I'm sure they will like it." Kane casually let a still pissed off Bossee know. She wasn't tripping on the body or the place he had gotten for the girls, it was everything as a whole Kane did that kept her temperature hot.

Torrica peeped the odd vibe in the room as she and her twin Trendini walked in his office. Kane was everything that Torrica wanted in a man, handsome, wealthy, and street all at once. Her womanly area purred every time she was near him and she found herself lusting after her boss' husband openly. Making sure to seductively lick her lips, she pretended that she didn't pick up Bossee being pissed off.

"Hey, Kane we took care of ole boy like you asked," Torrica said in a cute tone as she flopped in a chair in front of Kane's desk.

"Yeah, and the goon you was supposed to send with us didn't want to do any dirty work so Torrica shot em, and I chopped his ass up," Trendini spoke boldly. Torrica was a gunner but Trendini was the real killer. She had no problem chopping a nigga up with her bare hands.

Kane looked at them and they still had on their blood-stained clothes. Their hands were clean, but Kane could see blood spots on their face and in their hair, letting him know they were really with the business.

"Damn, I guess I'ma have to get rid of them niggas, I don't need nobody on the team slacking," Kane expressed.

"I told you stop trying to add niggas on the team, that was the whole point of starting a female crew," Bossee chimed in and said, kind of hitting one of Kane's nerves. He hated when she didn't trust his judgment.

"Well, I'm sure boss man knows what's best for us. Ain't that right, Kane?" Torrica said in a sassy tone, causing Bossee to dart her eyes straight at her and then she looked at Kane.

Kane looked at Bossee. He knew what was best for him, so he responded accordingly.

"I know what's best for us, but Bossee knows better before me. She runs this camp. So, look, for now on I'm going to have y'all meet somewhere else, no more dead bodies at the crib." Kane passed each of them a white envelope filled with money.

Bossee wanted to say so much but she kept her cool. They were in a business meeting and Kane answered Torrica to her liking so she kicked back and let him do his thing. However, Bossee did take notice that Torrica was flirting and it wasn't the first time. So, she made it a mental note to check her the next time it happened.

CHAPTER SIX

Later that night

Bossee was so glad to be out the house and away from Kane for a while so she could get her thoughts together on her personal life. No lie, she loved Kane with everything in her, she just sometimes felt like he didn't respect her. That was more hurtful than anything. She was his first lady and sometimes she felt like she was just his baby mama. True they were married, but sometimes it felt like they weren't.

It had been so long since Bossee had hit the streets of LA. The Lakers were playing against Golden State and Bossee and her cousin, Tosha, had courtside seats.

"Niggas is out tonight, I hope I snatch me a baller!" Tosha shouted.

Tosha was one of Bossee's older cousins and one of her favs. She was a hustler but she wasn't in the dope game, but her and Bossee clicked outside of their separate lives. She kept her a baller sugar daddy that did anything she asked. That's how she came up on courtside tickets that were five grand each.

"I just want to watch the game and get a drink. I ain't worried about these niggas," Bossee expressed as she looked out the window.

"You better! After what you told me. I can't believe you think Torrica feeling Kane. I know she wild but she ain't that wild," Tosha expressed as she found a lot to valet her car.

"I hope she ain't that wild because I'll drag her ass."

Tosha laughed, "my motherfucking cousins are crazy! Well, fuck that bitch then; she young, dumb and full of cum. They see a nigga like Kane and think they can handle all that and then some. But Kane a different kind of nigga. You gotta be a strong bitch like you, to rock with him!"

"You damn right cuzzo."

The ladies stepped out and Tosha paid the valet driver. The girls headed to the V.I.P line of the Staples center. They were inside and in their seats within thirty minutes. The stadium was live and loud as hell, but the girls were hyped to see the game. So, they enjoyed the preshow while sipping their drinks. The girls took pics and had their Instagram stories going. They felt like celebrities because they were surrounded by so many.

Bossee was feeling a little tipsy so she sat her drink by her foot so that she could take a break. No sooner than she sat it next to her suede heels, the guy next to her kicked it over by accident, spilling liquor all over her expensive shoes.

"Excuse me, but you just kicked my drink over all over my shoes," Bossee expressed to the man sitting next to her.

"My bad, Miss Lady, I didn't mean to. These courtside seats don't give you any space," the guy expressed as he looked down at the spilled drink.

He reached into the box of food that he was holding and pulled out a napkin. She declined it. She knew using paper towel on her heels would ruin them more.

"I'll be back Sha, this nigga den wasted drank all on my shoes."

"Okay girl, I'll be right here talking to him," Tosha flirted with the older white man that was sitting next to her.

Bossee made her way through the crowd in the halls of the Staple center until she finally found the bathroom. Thankfully, there wasn't a line because a lot of people were in their seats. So, she went in and used the bathroom. She reached into her handbag and pulled out a piece of cloth that she always kept in her purse. She dabbed her shoes and the wet spots on top of her foot.

"Now I'ma need another damn drink. A bitch got money but not for no thirty-dollar drinks," Bossee mumbled as she bent over and wiped her feet.

After emptying her bladder, she washed her hands and reapplied some pink lipstick to her lips.

When she stepped out the bathroom, the man that had wasted the drink onto her shoes was standing in front of the bathroom with a smile and a cup of brown liquor in his hand.

"I'm sorry for messing up your pretty, little shoes. I can't take you out to replace them right now, so I replaced your drink."

Bossee refused the drink.

"Nah, I'm good. You probably put some molly in that one."

She crossed her arms as she checked him out. She hadn't noticed who she was sitting next to until that very moment. It was her crush from high school, his name was Rory.

"Well, I can walk you to the bar and get you another one since you think I'm that kind of nigga," he shrugged his shoulders.

"Not to change the subject but I remember you… your name is Rory, you went to Westwood;

you used to play ball," Bossee smirked as she eyed the ice in his Rolex watch.

From the looks of it, he was getting money. She didn't know if he was still balling or selling dope. Either way, she could tell that he was paid.

"Used to is right, I'm an entrepreneur now. But damn, I'm sorry I don't remember you," he truly expressed while gazing at her.

"I'm sure you don't, I was a nobody… a nerd."

"Well you're looking like somebody right now, beautiful. You want to go get that drink or what?"

"Yeah, sure. I don't see why not. My name is Allaysia since you don't remember me," she extended her hand.

She decided to give him her real name instead of the nickname that Kane had given her.

He grabbed her hand and kissed it lightly.

"That's a pretty name," he said.

After he bought her another drink they went back to their seats. Bossee enjoyed the whole game but she was ready to turn it in once the game was over. As she was standing to leave, Rory grabbed her attention as they were making their way up the stairs to exit.

"I don't want this to be our last time seeing each other, you want to exchange numbers?" he asked with his hand on the small of her back.

"Yeah, sure. Give me your number and I'll send you a text later with my number."

She handed him her phone and he put in two numbers.

"Text them both, and don't forget."

"I won't…"

When Bossee made it home, it was midnight. The house was silent, and she was glad. Her daughter was with her mother, and she assumed Kane was gone so she headed to her bedroom and stripped out her clothes. She took a quick shower and got in bed naked. She laid in the dark listening to music on her phone looking at pictures in her phone from the game. She hadn't had so much fun like that in a long time and she wasn't going to let it be her last. That's when she remembered she had seen Rory and had his number.

Bossee had never cheated on Kane, but she felt like with the way that he was messing with bitches behind her back, she needed a back-up man. She couldn't believe the man she crushed on for years, was now digging her. Bossee wasn't always a bad bitch, at one point she was a nerd and didn't have any friends. But she told herself that once she turned eighteen, she was going to transform, and she did. It was no wonder why Rory didn't remember her because she used to be skinny, now she was stacked in all the right places. Her acne was gone, and she no longer wore baggy clothes and braces.

She went to his number and sent a text to both the numbers that he had given her. He only answered on one.

Rory: Thank you for texting me, Miss Lady. I'm sorry I don't remember you from high school but I'm going to look in my yearbook.

Bossee: Its cool, and yeah you do that. But I look nothing like I looked in the year book.

Rory: "I'm sure you were still as beautiful as you are now. I know it's too soon, but can a nigga take you out to lunch or something tomorrow if you are free?

Bossee smirked and then thought about the texts that she had saw in Kane's phone. As many women as he was trying to meet up with, she took that as a pass for her to go on a date.

Bossee: Sure… I'll be free between eleven in the morning until two. I have to get my daughter from school at three.

Rory: Bet. Pick a place and let me know, I'll meet you wherever.

Bossee: I got you…

Bossee deleted their messages and slid her phone on the charger. She drifted off to sleep feeling good knowing that if Kane didn't work out, she could get another nigga that was possibly better than him...

CHAPTER SEVEN

The following day...

Trendini and Torrica sat in front of their next victim's house, scoping out the place. Word was, the man they were looking for was the man in the streets. His name was Weedo, and he had that name for a reason. Weedo was the Kush plug. He was moving it by the pound. The streets thought that there wasn't any money in selling weed when medical marijuana shops were popping up everywhere and letting weed go for the low. But Kane knew it still sold. Everyone wasn't feeling that medical weed, so they were still looking for that fire on the streets. However, Kane had been trying to contact him but Weedo had been brushing him off, and he didn't like it. Therefore, it was the twins' job to get him to be down with Kane or knock him off and take his connect number from his cellphone. The twins had it all set up, but they had to make sure the nigga was really at home.

The two were sitting in a black on black Bentley with dark tinted windows. *R.I.P ARETHA* by Big Dreezy was playing low in the background as they passed a blunt back and forth with each other. Trendini knew they would be sitting there for a while, so she sparked a conversation with her twin.

"Sis, what's the deal with you, man? You trying to push up on our cuzzo husband? You wild, sis," Trendini hit the blunt hard and then passed it to Torrica.

"What? I was only stating facts, he is the boss, not Bossee. She just got the name, but she ain't no boss of me," Torrica hit the blunt and gazed out the window.

Torrica and Bossee were first cousins and grew up in the same house. Torrica always hated Bossee's bossy ways and was starting to feel like she was taking her name too far. She had only been working with Bossee for a month and already felt like she should have Bossee's spot. However, she didn't speak on it for the sake of her bag. Kane was breaking them off numbers that she hadn't seen in a while so she was going to play her hand with Bossee for as long as she could stand it.

"You and Allaysia need to kill it with the ego shit. You almost at a million dollars in a month. Be humble, twin," she took the blunt from Torrica's hand.

Torrica tossed up one finger and waved it, dismissing Trendini.

"Yeah, aight." she answered nonchalantly.

"AND STAY AWAY FROM KANE, SIS," she said boldly, making sure her sister heard her loud and clear.

"Trust me, that nigga for everybody," she shot back.

"Everyone but you."

At that moment, the girls saw a white Benz pull into Weedo's driveway. The girls immediately forgot about what they were talking about and got into beast mode. Trendini looked through her binoculars and watched Weedo walk into his house with a woman and two kids. The girls assumed it was his wife and his kids, and they were glad that they were with him.

“It’s go time,” Torrica expressed as she pulled her pistol from her handbag and stuffed it in her waist.

The two stepped out and the truck that was parked behind them doors opened. It was two of Kane’s goons, and Weedo’s big brother, Sharm. He was the girls pawn and ticket to the pounds. They knew using him as bait would have Weedo singing like a bird and dying to get down with Kane.

“Walk your stupid ass ahead of us and don’t run. If you do I’ma shoot your ass,” Trendini gritted at Sharm.

He frowned but did as he was told. They walked up to the door and Sharm used the key he had to his brother’s house.

“Stay out here with this nigga. I’ll tell y’all when we need him,” Torrica said to the goons.

They nodded and pointed their guns at Sharm.

The girls walked into the house and headed up the stairs. They could hear children laughing and a woman talking. Trendini went to find the kids and the wife while Torrica went to find Weedo. She walked into their master bedroom and found Weedo in their bathroom, doing a line of coke. She watched him take a long line to the nose and then close his eyes. She walked into the bathroom and pointed her gun at his forehead. The cold feeling of the tip of her gun made his eyes open right up. He knew that feeling from anywhere, now his next thought was, *who knows where I lay my head at night?*

"Yo, bitch! Who the fuck are you?" he shouted with spit flying from his mouth.

"Your worst motherfucking nightmare, bitch. I heard you didn't want to get down with my Boss Kane, so I thought I'd pay you a visit."

"Oh, so the nigga that pussy he send his bitch and not show up for himself. Well, tell that nigga I said suck my dick and he ain't getting my plug nor am I getting down with him and some bitches. He can take his country ass back to South Carolina with that shit because we don't do that shit here in Cali!" he spat boldly.

Torrica took her pistol and hit him across the face with it. Weedo grabbed his face. He was so livid that he tried to lunge at Torrica but she shot him in the leg. Weedo shouted.

"You want to play games, nigga. Okay, walk your ass downstairs, I got a nice game for you to play."

Bloody and hurting, Weedo limped down the stairs with a gun pointed to his back. Torrica tied him to a chair and then called the goons to bring his brother in. Then she called Trendini and told her to bring down the wife but leave the kids in the room.

A look of shock rushed across Weedo's face when he saw his brother and the two goons walk in.

"Brooo, you snitched me out?" Weedo asked as he made eye contact with his brother.

He felt betrayed that his brother would rat him out.

"Nah, they found me and told me that if I didn't take them to your house they was going to kill me and my kids," Sharm admitted.

"You let a bitch talk you into setting up your own brother?" he frowned at Sharm.

"Tell em why you agreed to bring us to where him and his wife laid their head at night. You've come this far. You might as well tell the truth," Torrica spat with a smirk on her face.

Torrica looked over at Weedo's wife crying her eyes out.

Torrica laughed.

"I don't know why you crying bitch. Why don't you tell em," she raised her eyebrow.

"Tell me what, Ashlee?" Weedo asked his wife. The tension in the room got thick as thieves in the night.

"Th-th-they knew I've been fucking your wife, bro. I knew you would kill her man. I couldn't let you kill her," Sharm said.

"You what!? Ashlee, how could you!" Weedo shouted.

"I'm sorry! But you were never here for me, your brother was!" Ashlee shouted.

"Alright, enough with the fucking drama. Weedo, you already made up your mind, so what you wanna do Sharm? You can off this nigga, tell us who the connect is, tell us where the stash, and then you can live with this bitch. Or I just off all y'all niggas and be done with it,"

Torrica spoke coldly as she looked Sharm in the eyes. She could see the scared look in his eyes. He knew all his brother's connects and had a key to his warehouse where he kept his product. Torrica knew that look from anywhere so she knew he was going to choose up on his brother.

"Ashlee, do you love me?" Sharm asked Weedo's wife right in front of him.

The plot was thickening and Torrica and Trendini were intrigued.

"W-what?" she stuttered as she looked between Weedo and Sharm.

"You heard me. It's over now. Now tell me you love me and our baby growing inside of you so we can move on with our lives. This is our chance to be together."

"Hurry up muthafuckas we ain't got all night. Do you love this nigga or what, Ashlee?" Trendini asked as she pointed her gun at Ashlee.

"So, this how we going out, bro. Really?" Weedo expressed as he shook his head.

"Yes Sharm, I love you!" she shouted out while sobbing.

Torrica handed Sharm a gun while guns were still drawn on him, just in case he tried to make a stupid move.

"You outta here, bro," Sharm let off three shot.

Two to his brother's chest and one to his head. Sharm dropped the gun to the floor while Ashlee cried out. He reached into his pocket and handed Torrica a key.

"You got what you came here for now leave us alone."

Torrica nodded, "we'll send the clean-up crew, you might want to take the kids out the back and go. We'll be in touch," she said.

The twins and the goons walked out the house and headed to their cars. When they got in the car, Trendini couldn't help but to burst out in laughter.

"Bitch your messy ass plan worked, I can't believe it!" she shouted as she lit her blunt.

"You be talking shit about me being nosey and being messy, now that shit paid us off. Kane is going to be proud of us and is going to give us a fat cut!" Torrica boasted.

She was doing all she could to show Kane that she could do the job better than Bossee...

CHAPTER EIGHT

"Nezzy, bitch I'm telling you, he off'd his own brother, we cold blooded," the twins said in union as they filled Neezy in with their latest licks.

Neezy continued packing the work Kane had given her to ship back to South Carolina. She listened as she vacuumed sealed the bricks, with a blunt hanging from the side of her lips. Nezzy has a tight schedule to get the drugs to South Carolina so she remained focused. She oversaw all shipments, so she had been really busy.

"Oh, this bitch ignoring us," Torrica said to her twin as she snatched the blunt from Neezy's lip. Again, she paid them no mind as she did her thing. Neezy knew the girls didn't mean anything by their words. The three of them had gotten close over the last few weeks because of their positions.

"You know that bitch can't work and trip. We have the easy job," Trendini spat jokingly.

Over the next hour Neezy had put everything in place for the shipment. This was her first one to South Carolina and even though it came second nature to her, she was nervous. She didn't want to let Bossee or Kane down or get them in any trouble.

"Okay, so I'm out y'all," Neezy said as she watched the goons take the last few boxes and put them in the truck.

Neezy had a knack for hiding drugs and moving them. With this shipment she had five hundred bricks stuffed inside of one hundred hospital beds. Nezzy's father owned a supply business that he let her move dope around with as long as he got his cut. He supplied equipment for nursing homes across the country. So, she did all the paperwork, so it looked legit to travel across the globe on a private business flight. She had it wrapped correctly so it would never be detected by K-9 dogs or when being scanned during X-Ray. She even went a step further and recruited her own security at a certain private airport company to make sure things went smoothly.

Neezy entered the van with the workers and took the thirty-minute ride to the airport.

"It's showtime," she said out loud to no one as she stepped out on the tarmac.

Kane and Bossee didn't even know how she would get the coke there because it wasn't their business. She kept her routes to herself, as long as the money was correct, she was with it.

Neezy made her way onto the spacious plane and got comfortable. The OG Kush she smoked on the way had her relaxed and focused. She busied herself in her phone, texting her contacts in South Carolina, to ensure that everything was in place.

"We are now prepared for takeoff," the intercom blasted the pilot's voice.

Neezy's plump lips foamed into a smile because she knew that she had pulled off the shipment.

The flight from L.A to South Carolina was five hours. She laid her seat back and closed her eyes thinking about the million dollars she had just made. The five-hour flight seemed like an hour to Neezy.

She had fallen asleep within thirty minutes of takeoff so she wanted to freshen up. She went into the bathroom and was getting herself together when her iPhone chimed. It was from Askaria Bitch, she was in charge of the traps, in and out of state.

Askaria: I'm in place so hurry up

Neezy: Bet! I'm still on the plane

Neezy shot a text back quickly. She grabbed her belongings and fastened her seatbelt as instructed by the pilot.

The plane descended, and Neezy was more than ready to finish the job. When the plane landed, she made her way to the workers that were waiting for her. After giving them instructions, she made her way to her awaiting car. Askaria was waiting in the back seat with a smug look. Askaria always had an attitude, and she wasn't in the mood to work so her attitude was on fire. However, Nezzy didn't know that because they weren't familiar with each other so she snapped as soon as she got in the car.

"Bitch, what the fuck is your problem?" Neezy asked as she lit a pre-rolled blunt.

"Bitch? Who said I had a fucking problem?" Askaria yelled as she rolled her neck and moved her arms around, hitting Nezzy in the face.

The fast hand gesture sent an already irritated Neezy into beast mode. With the blunt still in her hand, she grabbed Askaria's hair and slammed it against the window, knocking Askaria to sleep immediately.

"I'm not about to argue with no little ass dumb bitch," Neezy huffed as she watched the beds with the coke being place inside the truck. The truck had *Lòpez Long Term Supplies* on the side of it. She had everything in place and she wasn't about the let anyone get her jammed on some bullshit.

"Everything good?" the driver, Tom, asked as he pulled off.

Nezzy smoked her blunt while she cracked up laughing at Askaria's ass still being knocked out cold.

"Next time fix your face, hoe. Don't nobody got time for that bullshit," she voiced as watched the country roads of South Carolina.

They pulled up to the warehouse that Askaria was in charge of. It was surrounded by just trees with nothing else around. Nezzy slapped Askaria so hard that she jumped up in a panic.

"We are hereee," Nezzy sang.

Neezy could tell Askaria was dizzy and it made her laugh. She stepped out of the truck and FaceTimed Bossee to let her know that she completed her task.

"Yeah?" Bossee's face and voice popped on the screen after the first ring.

Bossee liked that Neezy could hold her own, but she was nervous about this trip. A lot of drugs was involved, and a loss right now wasn't what they needed.

"I'm here. Girl, and tell me why I had to knock Askaria's ass the fuck out. That bitch got an attitude problem and you know I don't play that shit when I'm in gangsta mode," Neezy popped off, shaking her head.

"BITCH, YOU GOT ME FUCKED UP!" Askaria shouted as she ran up and punched Neezy in the back of her head.

The hit caused Neezy to drop her phone and tumble forward.

Neezy could hear Bossee yelling in the background but she was more focused on beating Askaria's ass. She turned on her heels quickly and started to throw punches. Not many of the hits connected with Askaria but it was enough to get her to back up some. Askaria stood back to get in a fighting stance. She swung wildly, hitting Neezy in the face twice. Neezy used her weight to overpower Askaria when she grabbed and threw her to the ground.

She slapped and punched Askaria all over her face. Bossee was still yelling for them to stop from the phone on the ground. The girls didn't stop, they just kept trying to kill each other. Askaria finally had gotten on top of Nezzy, she clawed at Neezy's face. She didn't notice the can of mace until it was too late. Nezzy pulled it out her bra and sprayed Askaria. The string pepper had them both coughing but Neezy still gained control of the fight.

"Bitch!" Nezzy yelped before she punched Askaria in the eye, temporary blinding her.

Neezy grabbed her purse that was a few feet away from them.

"I'm going to show you who's really with the shits, TODAY," Neezy seethed as she grabbed a bottle of water and taser from her purse.

The workers were under Neezy's and Askaria's orders so they didn't stop the girls. They just looked on, trying to see what was going to happen. Dashing the water all over Askaria's upper body, she took her taser to the side of her neck.

"Aarrrrrrrrah!" Askaria croaked loudly. The voltage sent so much pain through her neck and face that she couldn't say anything else. Her body fell on the ground and it sounded like a bag of potatoes. Her body still shook for moments after falling, and Nezzy looked on as she took her last breath.

"Now bitch, look what happened," Neezy bragged, not really caring that she had killed her.

"Aye, clean this up, and take the work inside," she barked orders out to the workers who all looked on in shock.

"Neezy, what happened?" Bossee who was still on FaceTime screamed.

"I killed her stupid ass!" Neezy spat, still out of breath from the fight. She was pissed she had to roll around on the ground in her ten thousand-dollar Fendi outfit.

"Get rid of the body Neezy. Damn, I sent your ass thinking you're the quietest and you still end up with a body! Now I gotta figure out what to tell her damn girlfriend," Bossee expressed.

"Oh, and since you killed the bitch, you're picking up her damn slack!" Bossee continued and then hung up on Neezy.

"Shit, more money for me!" Neezy beamed.

She went on about her business with getting the work inside the warehouse. After introducing herself to the distributors she assigned them each their packages. Neezy collected the money from each worker and ran it through the money counter.

"Damn, it's a million-dollar day!" Nezzy gushed out loud.

She looked at her iPhone to make sure she was on schedule, she was flying back to Cali tonight.

"Wrap it up boys. We are finished here," Neezy hollered at the workers.

She was anxious to get back to show Kane and Bossee that she still had it. Neezy had a point to prove, even if she had to fuck the rest of those bitches up. The only person she felt she owed loyalty to was Bossee. Nezzy never got along with other females most of her life. She had a goal to get filthy rich, retire, and move back to Mexico with her family before she was thirty-five, and she was already thirty. She vowed no one would get in the way of that, and she knew Bossee was with her. They had been girls forever, and the same type of people, boss bitches.

CHAPTER NINE

Bossee sat in the deli where she was supposed to meet Rory, in deep thought. She couldn't believe Nezzy had killed Askaria. The shit had her mind blown, now she had to figure out what she was going to do with Equadree. She had known her since middle school and she trusted Bossee to take care of her girl while they worked separate missions, now she was gone. It was hard for her to pick sides because they were both her friends. *These bitches are getting out of hand,* Bossee thought to herself as she stared off in space.

She knew all the drama was spiraling because of greed. Each girl had their own agenda to knock one another off the map and Bossee knew that. That's why she stayed behind the scenes and watched the cash flow in. *We're going to have to have a meeting about loyalty,* she thought. Nezzy was her girl and she knew that was why she felt like she could do what she wanted, but that shit had to stop.

"What's up Miss Lady, something on your mind?" Rory snapped Bossee out her daze. She looked up and saw him standing over her with a smile on his face. She smiled back.

"Yes, but now that you are here, I can forget about it. How's your day going so far?" she sipped her lemon water.

Rory sat across from her in the booth and picked up a menu.

"It's better now that I'm here with you. So, I looked through my yearbook and I saw your picture. I do remember you…"

Bossee raised her eyebrow.

"Well, why didn't you ever say anything to me?" she asked.

"Because, I had a girlfriend back then. But I do remember you. You were somebody, you were one of the people that was always on the honor roll. Your picture was in the school newspaper every month. I remember one time reading the article about your achievements and was like damn she's going to be wifey material when she grows up."

Bossee laughed.

"Yeah right, you didn't think all of that, you're gassin," she shook her head.

"I'm not gassin, I'm for real. All the cheerleaders were jealous of you. They were smart but you were smarter. Remember, I was on the basketball team, and we all shared the same gym with the cheerleaders they talked about you all the time. Plus, my ex was a cheerleader. She talked about it all the time. They despised you. They even called you a green-eyed nerd."

He flagged down the waiter.

"Wow are you fucking kidding me?" she smirked and continued to shake her head. She remembered being called that many times in school.

"Yup, I played my cards all wrong in high school. Cheerleading got my ex nowhere, she lost her scholarship because she was doing drugs and I still stayed with her. I blew out my knee in college, so I stopped playing. While I was healing, she got pregnant, twice. One by me and one by some NBA nigga… But we're not together anymore."

"You came here with a mouthful, but I'm speechless."

"Don't be. You're nothing like those bitches from high school, you're different."

Bossee raised her eyebrow, "and what makes me different?" she challenged.

She wasn't easily impressed although Rory did have her attention. But she always wanted to know why men thought she was different from other women. She had her skeletons in the closet, so she felt no different from the next. Yeah, she knew she looked good and had a lot to offer, but she knew she was no different from any other female and she never portrayed herself to be.

"A lot sweetheart, trust me."

She figured she had caught him off guard with the question, so she let it go. Meanwhile, Rory's attention drifted off Bossee and to his ringing phone in his pocket. He looked at his phone and then he looked at Bossee with a smile.

"Excuse me, love, I have to take this call. Order whatever you want and order me a bacon omelet with a mimosa," he stood up and walked off.

Rory walked outside and answered his phone. He was furious at the caller, but he took the call anyway.

"Nigga, what the fuck you want?" Rory expressed in a low angry tone.

"It's day three nigga, what the fuck you gon' do?" the caller roared in his thick country accent.

"I ain't gon' do shit nigga. I know what you can do though, SUCK MY DICK!" he spoke loudly through the phone and then disconnected the call. When he turned around, he ran right into Bossee.

"Damn girl, you creepin' like a ghost," he said with a smirk.

"I just came out here to see if you wanted to hit this blunt before the food comes. Their talking about a forty-minute wait."

Bossee sparked up her blunt like a pro and blew smoke out her nose. Rory's mind shifted off the phone call he had gotten and focused on Bossee.

"And ya sexy ass smoke weed too, of course I wanna smoke with you."

The two walked by Bossee's Audi truck and faced a blunt. After they smoked, they headed back into the diner to eat. They ate a huge brunch and then walked back to the parking lot. Rory walked Bossee to her truck and opened the door for her.

"Damn, I haven't had a normal date like that in a while. I enjoyed ya company," Rory said as he grabbed Bossee around the waist.

His touch made her a little uncomfortable. It had been a long time since another man grabbed her by the waist like Kane did. He pulled her in for a hug and she wrapped her arms around his neck. She felt his hand go down her back.

"It was nice chilling with you too, I enjoyed you as well."

She felt him gently cuff her ass in his hand. She liked the feeling, but something was telling her it was too soon for any intimacy. She politely moved his hand and stepped away.

"I'm married, Rory," she spoke truthfully.

He stepped back and looked her up and down with a smirk.

"Damn, but I'm not surprised. You're definitely wifey material."

"I only went out with you because you're my friend, nothing more," she expressed in a soft tone.

"I understand, and I respect ya marriage Miss lady. I'm not going to make you do nothing you don't want to do."

"Thank you," Bossee said as she swept a piece of hair behind her ear.

"I got some tickets to the Bulls Vs Laker's game at the Staples Center again in two weeks. This time it's in the skybox. I'd like to take you with me, you know, as a friend."

"I'd like that, I love basketball and the Lakers are my team."

"Aight bet. Since I know I can't pick you up from your house I'll text you my address and you can meet me at my condo."

"Okay, so you single-single, inviting me over," Bossee laughed.

"Yup, single until I can have you," he gave her a seductive smile.

"Whatever, boy. Text me."

She gave him a friendly hug and then hopped in her truck. She quickly brushed Rory off her mind and headed to their new trap mansion to deal with her drama with the girls...

*****

Bossee sat in the white room of their new trap mansion sipping red wine looking at her gang, the Bitch Gang to be exact. She called a meeting with the girls without Kane to blow the news to them about Askaria. She knew it couldn't be a secret, so she wanted to be the one to share the news. She really didn't know how the girls would feel about the situation, especially Equadree, and she was hoping it didn't call any friction amongst them all.

"Where is Torrica? Her ass is always late. We always got Ying and not Yang," Bossee joked as she gazed at Trendini with a smirked.

Trendini shook her head and smirked as well, her twin was always late.

"She said she was leaving the salon thirty minutes ago. She had to get her wig tightened up, we stepping out after this," Trendini said.

"Well, I 'll wait five more minutes and that's it."

Three minutes later, Bossee heard the house alarm beep letting her know someone entered the front door. She then heard heels clicking her marble floors.

"Bitches, I'm here. Where y'all at?" Torrica said loudly through the house.

Nobody responded and let her find her way through the house. She had finally found them. Torrica walked in looking like a celebrity with her bright yellow wig and D&G sunglasses. They were laced in diamonds and they matched her blinged-out designer stilettos.

"Damn, you and Kane built this big ass house like a maze. You saw me on the cameras on your phone, you should have met me at the door," Torrica said slightly agitated.

"Bitch, sit down. You found your way, and take those sunglasses off in here so we can see your eyes," Bossee shot at her.

Torrica flopped on the couch next to her twin and snatched her shades off. She pulled a blunt from her Chanel handbag.

"Is it cool with you Bossee, since you boss everything. Can I light this?" Torrica asked with a smirk.

"I'm glad you know I'm the boss, bitch. And yeah you can light your shit a long as I hit it. You know this a weed smoking house. But now that you are here, I want to get things started. Askaria is dead, her and Nezzy got into it on a drop and she took her out in self-defense. She's not here because of that because she does feel bad about the situation. But none of this is not going to affect us in no way. However, I need y'all to chill out with your egos. If we're going to be a team, we gotta learn to all get along no matter what. We can't be killing each other, we're not the enemies."

"Wait, what the fuck did you just say? I thought you said she got held up at the airport that's why Askaria not here," Equadree stood to her feet with a mean mug on her face.

"You just going to sit there all casual and tell me by girl is dead and Nezzy did it?"

"I know that was ya girl but calm down and hear me out," Bossee stated in her usual chilled tone.

The twins looked from Bossee to Equadree. They could feel the tension in the room, but they kept quiet and observed.

"Nah, fuck that, Allaysia! You were supposed to keep her safe, you said Nezzy was cool!" Equadree shouted, calling Bossee by her government name.

"I wasn't there, E, but I was on FaceTime when it happened. Ya girl was tripping on Nezzy and they got into it and shit went too far. The shit was petty, but you know Nezzy don't play no games with the disrespect."

Before Bossee knew it, E charged at her.

"Bitch you got my girlfriend killed, I'm beating your ass and calling the police. I'll shut shit down!" E shouted as she attacked Bossee.

Both twins stood up and grabbed E before she could throw another blow. Trendini pulled her pistol from her purse and pointed it at E. Bossee stood to her feet and fixed her shirt.

"Bitch, I told you I wasn't there and now you wanna snitch? Take her dumb ass to the shed, twins, we about to handle this hoe," Bossee barked orders at Trendini and Torrica.

Torrica dragged E through the house while Trendini kept her gun pointed at her.

“Turn left and go through the kitchen, that’s where the exit is to the back yard,” Bossee said as she walked behind them.

She reached into her handbag that was on the kitchen counter and got her 9mm. She followed behind the twins while E yelled vulgar words at Bossee and the twins. The house was so far in the desert and they didn’t have any neighbors, so nobody could hear her screams.

“Allaysia, you’re going to rot in hell, you green eyed devil bitch!” E shouted with spit flying from her mouth as she spoke.

Torrica continued to drag her across the wet grass until they made it to the shed. Bossee helped Torrica tie E to a chair. Bossee looked around the shed and found a can of gasoline and some matches. She drenched E in gas and then lit a match.

As soon as the flames hit her skin, she started to scream in agony. They stood there and watched her burn until Bossee noticed the fire was starting to spread on the floor. There was a fire extinguisher so Bossee sprayed it on E and put out the fire. She was crisp burnt and unrecognizable. They walked out the shed coughing with black smoke over them.

"Damn, bitch did you have to set the bitch on fire, now my wig smell like a chimney!" Torrica said with an attitude as she dusted off her hair and outfit. Bossee and Trendini busted into laughter.

"Bitch, it's still early I'll drop you back by the shop and get your shit shampooed before we hit the club. You're just going to have to go wavy because them curls are out of here," Trendini said as they walked back towards the house.

When they walked back inside, they walked back into the kitchen. They were too dusty to sit in the white room, so they finished at the kitchen table.

"Thanks for y'all help tonight, it was so unexpected but we ain't going to let no snitches live. I'll call Kane and tell him what happened, and he will send somebody to clean the bitch up. Y'all go enjoy y'all night, and remember what I said… The team ain't the enemy, these niggas are." – She reached into her handbag and pulled out a wad of cash. – "That's ten grand, take it and have a good time y'all, for real."

The girls smiled.

"Awe shit, drinks on Bossee, it must be a good night," Torrica expressed with excitement.

After the girls left, Bossee locked up the house and went home. She called Kane and told him what happened and then she decided to text Rory to see if he was okay. She thought about when she walked up on him when he was on the phone at the diner, she noticed that he was angry. She wondered who was on the other end of the phone but decided to mind her own business.

What's up, Rory. I was just texting to see if you were ok. I can't wait to see you in two weeks.

Rory: It's all good. It's crazy I was just thinking about you. I can't wait to see you too.

Bossee smiled and then deleted their quick conversation. She couldn't lie, he was boosting her ego and she liked it. She was curious to where their relationship was going because things were getting really, rocky with her and Kane...

CHAPTER TEN

Two weeks later

Kane sat in his driver seat with his seat all the way back and his eyes closed. It was one in the morning and he was getting some top of the line head. He grabbed onto the back of her yellow weave and helped her go up and down on his stick. They were supposed to be staking out one of his enemies' trap houses, but he was so caught up in the pleasure. After drinking a half of bottle of D'usse, and taking two Xanax pills, his hormones were on the rise, therefore work could wait.

"Damn, daddy, this dick so biiiggg," she exaggerated as she ran her tongue up his shaft.

"I know, now keep suckin'," he expressed as he looked down at her.

Kane was on a mission with Torrica to see her gangsta in action. But, when she got in his car wearing a spaghetti strapped mini dress, he couldn't help himself.

Everything was spilling out from her ass to her titties. Not to mention for the first time he noticed that she was sexy as fuck. He had caught on in the past that Torrica was feeling him, but he had to feel her out first. Once he noticed her flirting, their eye contact became constant. Then when he had heard how her and her sister took out Weedo and the plan was her idea, he was curious about her gangsta. So, he texted her. Surprised that he had even texted her, Torrica took that as her moment to try and get into his pants and his world, and that she did.

"Shit, I'm about to cum," Kane said in a low roar.

Torrica took him into the back of her mouth and let him go to work on her throat. She was loving every moment of it. She felt like she had gotten her wish although she knew what she was doing was wrong. Knowing it was wrong actually turned her on even more. She anxiously waited for him to cum.

Within seconds, he let his babies go down her throat. Torrica sat back in her seat half satisfied because she wanted to fuck him too. But she didn't stress the fact because she knew that she would feel him inside of her in no time.

Kane got himself together and was back looking at the house in question. Torrica fixed her makeup and pulled down her skirt. Her breasts were exposed so she stuffed them back in her dress too.

"So that shit you did with Weedo was gangsta. That's the type of shit I like to hear. So, if you keep that attitude, I might bump you up a little bit," Kane said as he gazed at Torrica with his slanted brown eyes.

Torrica looked over at Kane and smiled, that was what she wanted to hear.

"Trust me, I'm confident in my work so I know that's going to be a done deal," she spoke with confidence.

"Bossee is my main bitch, my ride or die for real. But I can't lie I like you, and you bad as fuck while being on the frontline killing niggas."

He dug into his pocket and pulled out a stack of bills. He tossed it in Torrica's lap.

"Keep that mouth closed and you can get that on the side all the time."

Torrica ran her matte black stiletto nails through the stack of money with a smirk plastered on her lips.

"Shit, I can keep my mouth closed for free, and some dick, but I can use the extra money. I got you. Thank you."

"Aight, let's get out here and handle this nigga. If he ain't in there, murk everybody in that motherfucker, you hear me?"

He reached into his backseat and handed Torrica a fully loaded 12-gauge shotgun.

"Can you handle that?" he asked as he watched her eye the gun.

"Yeah, I've shot one of these before. I'm glad I brought my Nikes, this mothafucka big."

Torrica changed into a black sweat suit that was in her huge Louis Vuitton bag and a pair of sneakers. The two stepped out and headed towards the dark house that they had been watching.

Torrica walked on her tippy toes lightly once she and Kane reached the front of the house. She walked ahead of Kane, knocking on the front door. Kane looked at her as if she was crazy because he was confused why she was knocking on the door as if they weren't about to kill everything moving behind it.

"Yo, who is it?" a deep voice yelled from the other side.

"Hey, I just moved in two doors down. I think my breaker box tripped, because my lights aren't working," Torrica cooed from the other side, singling for Kane to remain quiet.

Kane stepped to the other side out of sight right before the door opened.

"Damn, you sexy as fuck," a short, chocolate dude said as soon as his eyes landed on Torrica.

"Oh yeah, so is my trigger finger," Torrica bossily stated.

Within a millisecond she had the shotgun pointed at the dude. Stepping forward she continued, "one funny move and I'm knocking your dreams out your head. How many people are in here?"

"J-j-just me and my two little cousins. Please don't shoot," the guy rambled shakily.

"Where the fuck is that nigga Rory, and don't lie," Torrica gritted at him.

"I-I don't know. He doesn't live here," the dude was almost in tears.

At that moment, Kane stepped behind Torrica proudly. She was turning him on in the worst way with her gangsta ways. Torrica turned the guy around quickly and pressed the gun in his back, letting him direct her further into the house.

"You're lying. Call them down now, and don't play no games!" she spat, taking the gun and chopping him across the head slightly. The house was quiet so she knew they would hear him if he called out. Torrica wasn't taking any chances searching the house, when they were outnumbered.

"Quince! Geno! Come downstairs right quick," the dude quipped as the pain in his head stung.

Kane could hear laughing and footsteps as they came downstairs, totally unaware of the danger a few feet from them. As soon as they saw their big cousin, Freak, being held at gunpoint, their eyes bucked wildly.

BOOM BOOM!

Torrica wasted no time popping the two young boys in front of their older cousin. Freak tried to rush Torrica, but she was quicker than him. She already had taken a step back and had the barrel of the gun aimed at his head.

"You gotta be quicker than that," Torrica declared as she squeezed the trigger, hitting Freak between the eyes close range.

His head exploded instantly but his body remained upright, until it finally fell backwards.

"Pussy ass niggas," Torrica huffed.

She turned to Kane because she noticed that he hadn't said anything since they got inside. When she looked back, he was standing there with a sexy smirk. Torrica followed his body with her eyes and noticed his dick was so hard that he had to adjust himself.

"Yeah, you deserve some dick after that, baby girl," Kane sang in his thick country accent that always had Torrica wet.

Walking over to her, he grabbed the back of her neck forcefully, tonguing her down like she was his wife. The thought of Bossee crossed his mind as he sucked and licked her lips, but Torrica's soft tongue pushed the thought away quickly. Pulling away from their kiss, Kane remembered he was now in a trap of Rory's.

Rory didn't want to get down with the moment, so he would kill everything around him, until he hopped on board.

"Now this nigga going to know who's boss," Kane said to Torrica.

"Now it's time for me to fuck you like the king you are," Torrica promised.

The pair exited the home without a care in the world. Kane helped Torrica put the gun in the back seat because they were now headed to their dumping grounds. The entire fifteen-minute drive Torrica teased him sexually. She connected her Bluetooth from her phone to his radio and played *Nympho* by Yung Bleu.

She unzipped her hoodie and allowed her 36 DD breast to bounce as she gave him a strip tease from her seat. Kane made sure not to swerve as much as he could, but it was hard keeping his eyes off Torrica's beautiful body.

Ass jumping, poppin' like a rubber band
Swinging on your trees like a jungle man
You will never ever need another man
I need your love, I need your love

Torrica mouthed the words to the song seductively as she rubbed her hands through her hair, and along her body. Kane passed Torrica the blunt as he pulled up to the dump off spot. He was almost tempted to fuck her brains out right there, but he wanted her for more than one round.

He hopped out of the car quickly after he popped the trunk. After he got the gun from the back seat, he put on his gloves and broke the gun down into pieces. He poured bleach over all parts then tossed them in the huge body of water. He had Torrica strip out of her bloody clothes and toss them as well. She slipped back on her dress and Gucci sandals, making sure she tossed her bloody Nikes too. They were back on the road within minutes.

Kane pushed the pedal as Torrica continued to grind in her seat to the music. They pulled into the Hyatt. Kane and Torrica checked in and went into the elevator. Once the doors closed, she stood in front him with her back towards him. She pressed her huge ass back on his dick and wined her hips.

"Damn your dick is hard already, baby," she said as she looked at him in the mirrors that were in the elevator.

Kane replied by sticking his fingers in her dripping wet box. She was soaked and her juices gushed out as Kane removed his fingers. He licked them clean as the elevator doors opened. Torrica was turned on, she wasted no time stepping out of the elevator and to find room 1111.

As soon as Kane slid the key in the door and pushed it open, Torrica grabbed his belt buckle. Opening it in a hurry, she grabbed his stick and slapped it on her face when she fell to her knees. Torrica sucked Kane's dick right there in front of the door. Taking her tongue, she ran it up and down his shaft. Her mouth was wet, so she turned her mouth into a vacuum and took him all in.

"Shhhhhhhhit," Kane hissed.

Torrica's head game was great. She kept whipping her tongue in circles as he was near busting in her mouth.

"Get the fuck up," Kane challenged.

He had to stop her before he let off again. He wanted some of her sweet tasting pussy, that was still on his mouth from the elevator. Torrica stood on command of his voice and hopped into his arms. As Kane walked her over to the bed they kissed like it was their honeymoon. Kane stopped in front of the bed and entered his eight inches inside of her pussy. He almost lost his balance. His intentions was to put the condom on that was inside of his backpack that he had with him, but Torrica had his head gone. He never fucked anyone raw besides his wife, but this felt right. She was tighter than he expected.

He slowly pulled out and rammed it back in with as much force as he could. Torrica looked him in his eyes as he did it again. Her fuck faces was pushing him over the edge. Torrica placed small, wet kisses on his neck as she kept her hands wrapped around his broad shoulders and neck. She matched his thrusts, letting her moans and gasps fall from her lips.

"Wait daddy, just hold me by my waist," Torrica hissed as she let go of his neck.

She leaned back and Kane kept his arm around her back. She rode his dick midair, swirling her hips in a circling motion. Kane watched as her titties bounced like water balloons and couldn't take it anymore. She had her hands behind her head and was pouncing with her hips.

"I'm coming. Fuck, Torrica," he bellowed hoarsely.

He couldn't pull out because he was to into the moment, so he fed her pussy his babies. He let Torrica go and she fell back on the bed on her back. He fell in top of her laughing at how she had just made him shoot off in a few minutes.

"Awww, we just starting baby," Torrica let him know as she wiggled from under him and got on all fours on the bed.

They had both popped a x pill earlier and it had them ready to fuck like crazy. Looking at her wide ass spread and her back perfectly arched was a blessing. His dick had its own mind and bricked up once again. Bossee was a beast in bed, but Torrica was on some porn star shit. Kane loved nasty sex since he was a jit, so he was with everything Torrica had to offer. *Fuck it*, he thought as he got behind Torrica and decided that it was his turn to give the best performance of the night. They fucked for two more hours. Kane didn't want to go home, but Bossee would bitch, so he busted Torrica down in the shower once more, then headed home to his wife.

CHAPTER ELEVEN

The following evening

Rory was furious at the mess he was stepping in when he walked into his trap house. Blood and brain matter was everywhere, and it had him sick. The bodies had been laid out for almost twenty-four hours so the smell really got to him. He raced to the bathroom and emptied the contents of his stomach. His nephews were dead, and it made him angry. His mother told him not to involve family and now he knew why.

"Aye yo cuhz, you okay in there?" one of Rory's workers asked through the bathroom door.

"Yeah, I'm good cuhz. Send one of the lil homies to get me a ginger ale from the store," Rory exclaimed through the door.

"You got it, boss." He heard his worker walk away.

Rory turned on the sink and threw water on his face and swished water around in his mouth. At that moment, he felt his phone vibrating in his pocket. He pulled it out and it was his worst enemy, Kane. He hated this nigga's guts and didn't even know when he came to L.A to try and take over, all he knew was at this point he wanted him dead.

"Yo, you came to my spot and killed my family, ya ass is dead!" Rory gritted through the phone in a rage.

"Catch me if you can, nigga. I told you to fuck with me or get knocked off," Kane laughed and then hung up in his ear.

"Grrrrrr," Rory gripped his phone and started pacing the bathroom.

His phone started to ring again. He was on the verge of getting mad until he saw that it was Allaysia. He didn't forget that he was supposed to be meeting her at his apartment in two hours so they could go to the game and he wasn't letting his situation stop him from stepping out with her.

"What's up Miss lady? You good?" he asked with a half-smile as he gazed at himself in the mirror.

"Yes, I'll be leaving my house in the next hour. I figured we could chill before we left to the game," her soft voice sounded like music to him.

"Yeah that's cool with me. I planned on having a driver take us to the game anyway so we could pregame and get as fucked up as we want. I had a long day, so I'm going to be drinking, drinking."

"Well, I'll be there soon to help you get out of that slump. You need me to bring anything?" she asked.

"Nah, my crib is fully stocked. Just bring ya sexy ass face, I miss it," he admitted.

"You always trying to make me blush, but I'll see you."

They disconnect their call

There was a knock on the bathroom door again.

"Aye boss man, we got your ginger ale and ya boys is here to get these bodies."

Rory sighed and walked out the bathroom. After taking a huge swig of the ginger ale, he was ready to get back to business. By the time the house was cleaned out, it was an hour and a half later. Rory told his crew that he would meet up with them about his next move and then he bounced.

He made it to his apartment in twenty. He had a chance to shower, straightened up his area, and make his crib smell fresh. Rory wasn't dirty or a nigga that liked clutter, but he was always in and out, so his house always smelled like nobody lived there, no smell. After everything was in place, Rory sat back blowing a blunt while waiting on Allaysia to arrive...

*****

Bossee had just came in from spending a day with her daughter and her mother, shopping and dining, now it was time for her to step out with Rory.

However, when she came home, Kane and his infidelities was on her heart heavy. He hadn't been home for days. Now, he was home showering and getting ready to hit the streets again. She sat at the end of her bed with Kane's phone in her hand once again.

Kane was cheating on her something serious and it had her burning up inside. She read through all his texts and with the number of bitches that he had ran through made her feel like she needed to go get tested for HIV.

"This nigga done fucked every bitch in L.A and then want to lay up with me every other night," she uttered as she scrolled through the text.

She hopped out the text and headed to his call log to see who the last person was he talked to. She figured whoever he talked to last was who he was going to link with. He was in the shower, so she knew that he was about to step out because he knew that she was.

She was on her way to the Laker game with Rory, but she wanted to solidify some shit before she left on her date. She saw that he spoke to a female named Lisa, but under her name was a name that made her heart sink.

"Rory," she said under her breath.

I knew he was into the business, she thought. Bossee sat the phone back on the bed and stormed into their master bathroom.

"Nigga you got me fucked up!" Bossee shouted, startling Kane a bit.

He was masturbating when Bossee had caught him off guard.

"What the fuck, Bossee. I'll be out in a minute."

"You going to fuck a bitch named Lisa? You been cheating on me with every bitch in the city? You got me all the way fucked up. I'm out, and I'm not coming back tonight. Don't miss me, you dirty ass nigga!"

"Aye, you need to calm the fuck down and stay the fuck out my shit. I'm not going to fuck nobody she wanna buy some dope! And if you stay out all night I'm beating the fuck out of you!"

"Fuck you, Darell Kane Smith, and kiss my ass. I'll see you in the morning and have my bread wrapped in a bow!" She slammed the bathroom door and went back into the room.

She grabbed her purse and bounced before Kane could catch her. She was cool on Kane and their marriage. She was going out and having a good time with her new friend Rory.

Bossee pulled out her driveway blasting, *Attention* by Moshaae. She was trying to get her mind off Kane's bullshit. She lit up a blunt and rolled her windows down and let the song take over her mind.

See I've been lonely for a minute, where you been at? You fucking with these bitches, I'm the one need yo attention. I got one question, can you say they beneficial? Can't be wasting all my time trying to show you what we can do.

How you let her get a feel for you, I can never understand. Hold a place in yo' heart, you supposed to be my man. Always talkin bout you fucked up, let another nigga luck up, you be ready with yo chest up, then we throwing off the man.

She didn't understand how he could cheat on her so excessively. She did everything a wife was expected to do yet he still stepped out on her. Not to mention she was the one that put his crew together and they were bringing in a serious cash flow for him. *I deserve better,* she thought as she got on the freeway.

Bossee pulled up to the address that Rory had given her and killed her engine. He lived in a fly ass condo that was in West Hollywood. It was on a low-key street where you could tell that not a lot of activity happened there because there were hardly any street lights. Bossee grabbed her handbag and stepped out her truck. She searched for his name on the buzzer and pushed the button next to his name.

"Take the elevator up, I'm in apartment 202," he said through the intercom then the glass door buzzed for her to open it.

She took the elevator to the only floor it had which was the second floor. She got off and noticed there were only three other apartment doors. She walked up to 202 and knocked. Rory opened the door with a smile on his face. He was dressed in a pair of Balmain jeans, a navy-blue short sleeved polo Ralph Lauren shirt, a few gold chains, and a purple Lakers snapback. He had on a pair of navy-blue Nike Cortez, which let her know off top he was a Crip. Bossee liked that. She loved a baller ass Crip nigga from Los Angeles that could still rock a pair of old school Nikes.

"Oh, you were serious when you said you were a true Lakers fan," he said as he let her step in.

She was wearing a yellow and silver custom-made sequin Lakers jersey dress. It sparkled so much it made her feel like royalty. The silver glitter thigh high boots fit snugly on her legs, with just as much sparkle as her dress. She wore her big hoop earrings, and Cuban iced out choker and matching bracelet.

"Yup, I told you. I don't play," she smiled as she watched him close the door and lock it.

"You look nice tho'. I see you don't play about your shoe game either."

He glanced at her boots. He liked a woman that could rock a pair of high thigh boots with class.

"I sure don't. It's rare you will see me in tennis shoes. Boots and stilettos are my thing."

She sat on his couch and started looking around. She couldn't lie, from what she could see his bachelor pad was fly and neat. His decor was blue and gray, and he had a huge aquarium of fish placed in the wall.

"Yeah, you can leave the tennis shoe wearing up to me."

He flopped on the opposite side of his gray sectional.

"My driver will be here in thirty minutes. You want a drink?" he asked.

"Yeah, as long as it's brown. I don't do the light."

He stood up and Bossee did as well. After they made their drinks in his kitchen they stood in front of his aquarium and made small talk while they waited. His driver showed up in exactly thirty minutes. Bossee finished off the remainder of her drink and popped a mint in her mouth.

Once Rory locked up his place, she followed him down the hall to the elevator. She peeped the cool little sway in his walk and the slight limp he had as she walked behind him. She assumed the limp came from his knee injury that he had told her about. *He got a big dick,* she joked in her head. She had a thing with the way men walked. She always knew a man that walked with confidence was definitely packing.

When they made it down and walked out the building, there was a black on black Bentley truck parked in the street with the hazard lights on. Rory grabbed Bossee's hand and escorted her to the car.

The car ride was a bit silent as they looked out the window at the city lights and listened to random music that was playing on a satellite station. Bossee was anxious to get to the game and feel the excitement. She loved basketball games. Ever since she was little, her father used to take her to all kinds of games. Football, baseball, basketball, and even hockey.

Twenty minutes later, they were in front of a packed Staples Center. All eyes were on them when they stepped out. With all the commotion and cars around them, people were gazing at them trying to see who they were and if they were celebrities. The two ignored the stares and made their way to the V.I.P line hand in hand. They were let in and escorted to a private elevator. There were a few people on the elevator with them. Bossee was trying to see who was coming in the same box as them but she realized when they got into their box, nobody was with them.

She looked around the exclusive box as good as she could. It was dark and had a club setting to it.

There was a fully stocked bar a small dance floor and a couch area. The DJ was playing music while the players were on the floor warming up.

"Where's the rest of your party?" she asked as she looked out at the players shoot the ball.

"We are the party. I got this for us to enjoy alone."

Damn this nigga balling like that? Bossee thought. *No wonder Kane probably want his head. But if he moves like this Kane ain't gonna ever touch this nigga.*

"Oh, well let's get the party started then," she strutted over to the bar.

They ordered hot wings and two bottles of D'usse. Bossee promised she wouldn't get too drunk, but the environment had her drinking blindly while she enjoyed the game.

"I bet you a hunnit the Lakers don't win!" Rory shouted at Bossee as he laughed.

He took a shot and slammed it on the table in front of them.

"Don't try to play me, Rory. I know my team suck, but they gone win and I'm not betting you," she sassed.

"Why not?" he asked.

"Because I don't have a hunnit."

Rory laughed, "bet them boots then. I know they costed more than a stack."

"I'm not betting my boots, crazy ass."

The buzzard rang and the Lakers had missed a shot. It was half-time so Rory went in for another shot. However, he noticed how close Bossee was sitting to him. She had one of her legs over his, slightly giving him a sneak peak of her white satin panties. Rory smirked. He figured it was just the liquor courage.

"You are sitting mighty close to me tonight," Rory gripped her thigh and massaged it, noticing she didn't budge.

"I know, I feel like I'm just getting closer to you every time we kick it."

She took her stiletto nail and ran it on both sides of his face. Ever since she told him she was married, he didn't try anything on her. But he knew the more they kicked it, the more she would come around. Rory was grown and knew when a woman wasn't happy in her marriage. They texted from sun up to sun down and she had no problem going out with him in public. He felt like if she was happy, she wouldn't be kicking it with him, even as a friend.

Rory gazed in her glossy green eyes.

"I could kiss your sexy ass right now," he expressed.

Her lips were so glossy and plumped, he wanted to suck on them.

"What's stopping you?" she smirked.

He moved into her space closer.

"You… being a married woman."

"You been holding my hand all night and didn't notice I wasn't wearing my ring."

Rory looked down at her small fingers and noticed she wasn't wearing her ring. He wasted no time pulling her closer and tonguing her down. Bossee felt her heart pick up as their tongues slow danced. She pushed him back slightly and placed her hand on his. She got up and sat on his lap with her back towards him. She guided his fingers to the back of her dress for him to unzip it.

Rory let her take the lead because he wanted to be sure she was ready for this. He slowly undid the zipper as she rotated her plump ass against his now rock-hard tool. As soon as the dress fell off her shoulders, Bossee stood up and it fell to their feet. She still had her back turned so all Rory could see was ass in front of him. She sidestepped out of it and turned around facing him, showing off her full, perky breast.

Bossee let him take in her body and watched as the fire jumped in his eyes. She kept her boots on, and saddled him like a pro, she took her time unbuckling his jeans, eyeing him sexually. Rory bit his bottom lip, right before he pressed her lips back into his. He lifted his bottom slightly so she could tug his pants and boxer briefs down. He had discreetly grabbed a condom out of his messenger bag that he had brought with him while her back was turned. He slid it on as they continued their kiss.

As soon as he finished rolling it on, Bossee propped both of her legs on his arm rest and slowly slid down his pole.

"Shhhiiittt… Allaysia," Rory sucked in a deep breath.

His eyes rolled back in his head and he damn near lost it. Bossee got in a rhythm and began to take them both on a sedated ride. Rory tried kissing her but Bossee was so in her zone. She grabbed his neck pushing him back, using it to help her keep her balance. She was now on her tippy toes in her boots, thrusting like she hadn't had dick in years. Bossee had blacked out to the point she was taking advantage of his dick.

Rory's lap was covered in her juices, he looked down in awe. He had never seen a woman get so wet in his life. Rory tried his best to stop the building pressure from releasing, so he had to stop looking down at her wet pussy.

"Nigga, you gon' make me cum all over your shit," Bossee growled.

She was doing all the work, but his long thick shaft was touching all her spots on the inside. She plowed her body faster now with her fingers twirling around her nipples while Rory massaged her clit with his fingers. She felt her nut coming and so did Rory. He pumped as best he could with her.

"Grrrrrrrrrrr…." they both let out at the same time.

They both were experiencing an out of body, soul snatching feeling. Bossee remained seated on him with his semi hard penis still inside. They were spent from the wild sex and could only gaze into each other's face.

"Damn, Allaysia, I wasn't expecting this tonight," Rory finally spoke.

Bossee got off his lap and stood in front of him in the nude. She picked up her dress and slipped it back on.

She then picked up her panties from the floor and stuffed them into Rory's bag like a souvenir. She kneeled and gestured for Rory to help her zip up her dress.

"I wasn't expecting that either, but it was special. I'm going to the restroom to freshen back up, you wanna go too?" she looked down at his limp dick still out his pants with the condom on.

He looked worn out, Bossee couldn't help but to smirk. She knew she had good pussy, that's why she never passed it around and didn't understand why Kane cheated. The same way she rode Rory, she did it for Kane when he was home.

"Yeah, yeah, I'm right behind you." Rory stood up and slid the condom off his dick. He fixed his pants and put the condom in a napkin and decided to flush it in the bathroom.

The two stepped out the private box and into the empty hallway. The game was back on so everyone was in their seats. They went into separate bathrooms to do their thing. Bossee came out first and started heading back to the box when she heard Torrica's loud ass calling her name.

"Bossee, Allaysia, bitch don't act like you don't hear me!" Torrica staggered over to Bossee struggling in her high heels.

"I heard you, Torrica. What you doing here?" Bossee asked uninterested and in a hurry. She didn't want Rory coming out the bathroom and Torrica saw who she was there with.

"Nahhh, bitch what you doing here? You here with Kane?" Torrica smirked and shifted her hips to the side.

"No, I'm here doing a drop off, so I'll check you later." Bossee tried to walk off but Torrica grabbed her arm.

"Yo hair bushy, and I know you ain't step out like that."

Torrica pulled up Bossee's dress causing her to react. She pushed Torrica away from her.

"Bitch, you ain't got on no panties, and you always wear panties. And, I know Kane ain't gonna let you come out with no draws. Don't ask how I know, but I heard y'all arguing about it one day. I ain't gon tell, I see you' bitch. You here with a nigga," Torrica winked.

She wasn't going to tell Kane, she was just going to use that to fuck with him some more.

"Bitch, you don't know my life. I'm here doing a deal on my own. Now carry on to where you were going," Bossee stated boldly.

"Okay, damn just dismiss your favorite cousin. I'll see you tomorrow then."

Torrica staggered off to the skybox that she was chilling in. She knew a couple NBA players and they always gave her V.I.P access.

"You know you ain't my fav, bye hoe," Bossee walked off and headed back to the box.

After sitting there for ten minutes by herself, having another drink and Snapchatting her experience, Rory came back. They didn't speak on what had just happened between them. They finished watching the game and had more drinks. An hour later, the Lakers had lost. On the car ride back to Rory's apartment, Bossee fell asleep in his arms. She was so drunk, she could hardly keep her eyes open.

"We here, Miss Lady," Rory said in her ear. Bossee sat up and stretched. They got out and Bossee walked over to her truck for her bigger hand bag she carried around with things she needed just in case she crashed somewhere. After she got her things, they walked into his building. She had plans on going to a room, but she decided to stay the night with Rory.

He grabbed two waters from his refrigerator and escorted her to his master bedroom. Instead of turning on the light, he turned on his TV. CNN came on at a medium tone. Bossee gazed at his king-sized bed and slipped off her dress and boots. He passed her a water and she wasted no time downing it.

"You can get in my bed if you want to. If you want me to respect your privacy, I can sleep in the living room, because I'm not letting ya drunk ass drive home tonight."

Bossee laughed.

"I'm not drunk but I wasn't planning on leaving. I want you to lay with me."

Rory slipped out his clothes, leaving on his black Versace boxer briefs, and slid under the covers with Bossee. He snuggled up behind her and wrapped his arms around her warm body. He hadn't had a moment with a woman like he was having with Bossee in years, and it felt right to him.

"You want to know the truth about me?" Rory asked Bossee as she laid there with her eyes closed listening to the TV.

She was already falling asleep until she heard his voice.

"Uh, yeah… Of course."

"I'm more than an entrepreneur, I sell dope…"

There was a brief silence between the two. Bossee wasn't surprised because she already knew. However, she was so relaxed in his comfortable bed, her mind zoned out for a second.

"Oh really, well thanks for telling me. You gotta do what you gotta do and it looks like it's working for you."

"Just know if this night goes further than fuckin' and friendship, I got you."

"I hear your Rory." Bossee fell asleep with his last words on her mind.

Before she knew it, it was morning. She looked over at Rory and he was still sleep, but she could hear her phone buzzing in her bag. She got out of bed and grabbed her bag. She found his bathroom and went inside. She looked at herself in the mirror and she was surprised she didn't look a mess. Her hair was fuzzy but thankfully she carried her flat iron everywhere she went. She searched his bathroom drawers and found a clean face towel and a brand-new toothbrush.

Bossee got herself together and stepped out the room to slip back on her dress. It was payday and she needed her money from Kane.

"You out of here, Miss Lady?" Rory asked as he sat up in bed.

Bossee gazed at him and bit down on her bottom lip. Sober and drunk, Rory was something to look at. She wanted to stay but she knew she had to go.

"Yeah, busy day. Text me later, I might fall back through."

"Aight, bet. Lock my bottom lock on the way out," Rory said as laid back down.

Bossee found her way out and did her walk of shame with confidence. She looked at the time and saw that it was ten in the morning. She was expected to meet Kane and the girls at their trap mansion at 10:30. The house was thirty minutes away from where Rory was located so she skipped going home and headed straight to her money...

CHAPTER TWELVE

After Bossee stormed out the house on Kane, it had him sitting back thinking about his actions. His plan was to come to California and take over the dope game, but the streets had him on some different shit. Bitches were feening for him left to right, and it was hard for him to turn pussy down. His ego, drugs, and his money wouldn't let him, now he was caught up with Torrica. Not only was she his worker, that was Bossee's first cousin.

Her seductive ways had him sucked in, and he felt like he had the situation under control. But then he remembered that he thought that she was pregnant. Either that, or the many drugs she was taken when they were together had her sick to her stomach. *I'ma have to start using a condom with this bitch,* he thought to himself as he threw money into his money machine.

After he ran the rest of his money through his machine, he sorted out money for each girl. He was appreciative of everything each one brought to the table, even though the situation with Askaria and Equadree was fucked up. He was all for taking niggas out, but not the ones on his team. He shook his head at the thought and moved on to sorting his money. After he sorted it, he wrapped each stack in rubber bands.

When he was finished, he heard a knock on the door. He knew it was Bossee, so he opened the door without asking who it was. When he opened the door, Bossee stood there looking like a goddess. Her face was unusually glowing, and her hair was jet black and straightened to the bone. She was still wearing her yellow and silver custom-made sequin Lakers jersey dress and boots.

"What's up, Kane? You gonna move out the way so I can come in?" she asked, snapping him out his thoughts.

Something about the glow in her face threw him off.

"My bad… But what's up with you? Your ass ain't come home last night," Kane followed behind her to his desk.

"I stayed in a hotel by myself. I'm not fucking with you right now. So, don't touch me." Bossee flopped in one of the chairs in front of his desk.

"Well if you not fucking with a nigga, why you here?" Kane shot back at her.

"To get my money…"

Kane smirked, "Why? You ain't did shit, so what you earn?"

"Excuse me?" Bossee raised her eyebrow.

"Nothin'..."

"Yeah, that's what I thought. Remember you are the cheater, not me," she shot back at him.

She hated when his ego got the best of him. But she knew he was only shooting shots because he was mad, he was caught and didn't know how to express himself. He was exposed and he didn't know Bossee's next move and it had him a bit scared. He had to admit he had been sloppy, but he was thinking about cleaning it up soon.

"Whatever, Bossee, you know I love your ass and I ain't cheating. I know you earned your cut too. None of this wouldn't exist without you. These your peoples."

"Whatever, nigga… You cheatin'..."

Bossee glanced at the money on the table. She could tell who's stack was whose, because this was their seventh payout since they started. Everything looked even until she looked at her stack, which was the bigger one… then she looked at the one next to hers. *Who the fuck is he giving a raise too?* she thought to herself. *I'm not even going to say nothing, I'ma just sit back and peep shit.* Before Kane could respond again, there was a knock at the door. Bossee smiled and stood up to open it because she knew who it was.

"Nezzy, bitch! Welcome back!" Bossee shouted as she bearhugged Nezzy.

"What's popping sis?" Nezzy said as she gave a heartfelt hug to Bossee.
She gave Kane a head nod as a gesture to greet him.

"It's payday, so I'm ready to blow the mall down. You coming when we finish up here?" Nezzy asked Bossee as another knock at the door interrupted their girl talk.

Torrica and Trendini walked in looking like models as always. Kane remained seated behind his desk, he was writing on a notepad each Bitch's name. He place their written names on which stack belonged to them. The girls were still greeting each other and speaking among themselves.

"What's good ladies? Your money is here, please find your names and take your cut. I want to personally thank you all for putting in that work for m… I mean for Bossee and I," Kane said grabbing the girls' attention.

"Welcome back Neezy," Torrica said laughing.

She thought it was funny that Nezzy had killed Askaria.

"Thank you," was Neezy's reply.

She wasn't about to go into the past, she was letting the dead remain there. Torrica was the first to go over and picked up her money off the desk. The girls all saw that hers was the biggest next to Bossee's.

"Why did she get a raise?" Bossee asked while looking over at Kane.

"T has been kicking in doors and dropping a lot of bodies. she earned it," Kane replied monotoned.

"Yeah, Bossee, I been kicking in doors, what you thought?" Torrica crossed her legs and rolled she eyes.

"So, I've heard…" Bossee left it at that.

She did agree with the amount of work she had been putting in, but not the amount of money he was giving her, but she let it go.

Bossee looked over at Neezy's crazy ass because she knew she didn't have all her marbles, but her face didn't give off any indication that she was mad about Torrica's cut. In Nezzy's mind, she felt like she put in as much work as Torrica and Trendini. Yeah, she was out for a couple weeks, but she was still doing her runs. Bossee reached over to her stack, picking it up, and the remaining girls did the same.

"Okay, now that that's out of the way, we have a busy schedule this month. Bossee will get with each of you and run everything down," Kane schooled them.

Nezzy was listening to Kane but she was watching Torrica's body language as he spoke. She had gotten close with the twins, but something was off and she couldn't place her finger on it. She made a mental note to keep an eye on everything.

"Bossee, let's hit the mall. I have a hot date tonight and a bitch needs to be fly," Nezzy said as she slapped fives with her friend.

"Damn, so we not invited or something," Trendini asked playfully.

They all hadn't done anything as a team besides work, so Bossee thought it would be cool to hang out.

"Shit come on. We about to be lit in the city, let's make it a girl's day," Bossee suggested.

She was excited to have what was left of the Bitch Gang together for the day. Bossee was really happy to be away from Kane's ass also. She meant what she said, she wasn't fucking with him right now.

After they left Kane, the girls went their separate ways. Bossee knew Kane was not coming home after the meeting so she used that time to go home and clean up. She still had on her same clothes from the night before so she needed a shower. She came straight from Rory's crib to Kane's meeting with Rory still all over her. She could even still smell the scent of his cologne on her dress. That was the real reason why she didn't want Kane to touch her.

As crazy as it sounded, she felt good sitting in front of Kane with another man still on her skin and on her mind. That was why she didn't even trip on him giving Torrica a raise. *This nigga can do whatever he wants,* she thought as she stepped in the shower. Flashbacks plagued her mind of Rory as she lathered her body with her coconut scented shower gel. *Damn, Rory fucked me like he loved me last night.* Bossee's mind rambled uncontrollably. She finished up her shower quickly and got dressed. She checked her phone and saw a group text from Nezzy and the twins.

Headed to the mall now y'all ~Nezzy

Bossee shot an *ok* back to them and finished getting her hair to straighten. Ten minutes later she was headed out of the door and to the mall. She saw Neezy and Trendini standing near valet as she pulled up a couple minutes later.

"Let's tear this shit down," Nezzy said as she clapped her ass laughing.

Nezzy was a party girl at heart so they all shared a laugh with her.

"Where's Torrica?" Bossee asked Trendini when she noticed she didn't see her.

"She said something about a job she had to finish, and that she will catch up with us at dinner," Trendini let her know.

Bossee gave a slight shoulder shrug, she respected that Torrica was in full grind mode.

The girl's walked in the mall with authority, and all eyes were on them. They paid no one any mind as they made their way through the mall in their own world. The girl's talked about everything except work as they went into several designer stores and cashed out. They gossiped about the drama on Instagram with Cardi B and Offset. They were now in Nezzy clothing store, resting their feet.

Nezzy owned several stores called *PIRL* meaning *Pretty in real life.* One of her *PIRL* workers came over to grab the many bags they had with them. The worker gave them each a glass of champagne.

"Cardi is right for leaving his ass," Trendini stated continuing their conversation they started before they sat down.

"Yeah, fuck all that. It's a difference between being a rider and being a dummy," Neezy spat her opinion, agreeing with Trendini.

"Ohhhh… Nezzy this is cute," Trendini yelped getting up and going over to a dress that caught her eye on the other side of the store.

"Kane cheating on me Nez," Bossee blurted out to Nezzy unemotionally.

Bossee had accepted the fact that her knight and shining armor had switched on her. She was pissed and hurt because they had been together for so long and had been through so much together.

"I went through his phone and found over fifteen different bitches," Bossee continued to put her friend on point about her fucked up marriage.

"Damn, Bossee! You don't deserve that shit. You're a good ass wife. You take care of Keyley, you get to the money, and you're bad ass bitch. I'm not the friend that's going to say leave your family, but I am the friend that's going to say, get your bag together. So, if you bounce on that nigga, you're good. I took this position with Bitch Gang because of you, so you know I'm rocking with you until the engine stop running," Nezzy compassionately expressed.

Bossee sipped her champagne as she soaked up the game Nezzy had kicked to her. She appreciated her words because she knew Nezzy was really a friend to her.

"I'm getting this dress y'all! What y'all over here talking about," Trendini boasted as she walked back over modeling the dress she had fell in love with.

She was in the dressing room up until then. The full lace see through dress was stunning on her body.

"That shit is all you boo," Neezy said ignoring her question asking about the conversation her and Bossee was having.

"Y'all, I'm hungry as hell," Bossee added gratefully that Nezzy kept their conversation between them.

The twins was her family and, she loved them with everything but she wasn't ready to put her home business on front street. She'd always been a private person, she and Nezzy just shared a special bond, the same bond that she lost with the twins while she was in South Carolina. She and Nezzy stayed in contact the entire time via FaceTime, so their relationship was stronger.

"I'm about to pay for this so we can dip," Trendini said not really paying attention to anything besides her reflection in the mirror.

After she changed and paid for her dress, they all gathered to leave. They had so many bags that Nezzy had her workers take them to their cars. They decided that they would eat at an upscale restaurant that was located inside the mall. They made their way over to the restaurant, enjoying the attention from some niggas yelling catcalls and saying how sexy they were. When they arrived inside the expensive restaurant and approached the hostess, Nezzy took the lead.

"Faazon, I know it's packed but my girls and I need a table, without the wait," Neezy cooed flirtatiously.

"Of course, Ms. Lopez," Faazon said as her ushered the ladies all back to a cozy table near the bar.

Nezzy gave him a couple hundreds and winked her eye as he made his exit back to the front. Shortly after, a short skinny white girl came over to take their drink and appetizer orders.

"Torrica just texted and said she's still caught up, but she will make it up next girls day," Bossee let them know.

She had texted Torrica and asked if she wanted them to order her anything because they had made it to dinner. *What kind of job is Torrica's ass on without me?* Trendini pondered to herself. They did all jobs together except for the one she did the other day with Kane.

At that moment, Trendini's stomach growling overpowered her thoughts about her sister. She was happy that the waitress came back with the appetizers and wine. The girls each spat off their food orders to Shelly the waitress, while munching on the bread and lobster rolls. As they were chatting and dining, Bossee received a text.

Rory: Can you wear some boots for me tonight?

Bossee's cheeks flushed red, she couldn't help the huge smile that spread across her lips when she read the text from Rory. The other girl's noticed the devilish grin Bossee displayed.

"Kane must be about to knock the dust off the pussy tonight, you smiling so hard," Trendini teased Bossee.

Nezzy knew that text couldn't have been from Kane, but she laughed along with the joke.

"Yeah, that nigga is crazy," Bossee fibbed as she went into a fit of laughter along with the girls. She knew Nezzy wasn't about to address it, and she's wouldn't either.

"I can't wait until I find nigga and be a boss ass couple like you and Kane, Boss," Trendini spoke sincerely.

She always like Kane and Bossee together, especially now with them taking over Cali as husband and wife. She was grateful to be a part of their squad and running up real money with them.

"Cuzzo you have no idea. Keep your eyes on the bag, fuck this love shit," Bossee said as she texted Rory back.

If I make it, I got you. ❤

"Yeah, it's always money over everything. Let's toast to that. To the Bitch Gang," Nezzy said raising her wine glass.

The girls followed suit after pouring more wine into theirs.

"To the Bitch Gang," they all said in unity as they clangged their glasses together, not aware of the chaos lurking, waiting to test their sisterhood.

CHAPTER THIRTEEN

One month later...

"You better bring your ass fucking home tonight ALLAYSIA SMITH!" Kane hollered in the phone with enough base to scare a grown man.

This was the new norm for them as of late. Bossee would deal with Kane only during business then disappear. She was never home when he got there, and it was starting to make him upset. He was screaming into the phone, leaving yet another voicemail. During the time with Bossee not being home, him and Torrica began getting closer, but his wife didn't notice. She rarely picked up her phone for him and he barely saw their daughter.

Kane knew he had to do something and fast before he lost his wife for good. Torrica was a cool fuck but he needed his wife, she was his whole heart. Torrica was becoming too attached to him but he knew he was the one to blame.

"I see you're still begging your wife like a little punk," Torrica sassed as she stepped back into the bedroom of the suite that they had been occupying for the last two weeks. Torrica knew Bossee wasn't worried about Kane since she saw her at the Staple Center, so in her mind he needed to just leave her ass alone.

"What I done told your ass about minding my damn business. Keep it up and your ass will be out of here! You need to be worrying about making an appointment to the clinic to take care of your problem," Kane cold heartedly yelled.

"MY PROBLEM? NIGGA, THIS IS YOUR FUCKING CHILD TOO," Torrica screeched loudly.

Her emotions had been out of whack lately, so the tears immediately poured down her face. Kane was unfazed by her tears and shooed her off with his hand. *This is why I need to get my shit together. Bossee wouldn't be doing all this crying and shit. What the fuck was I thinking?* Kane thought to himself. He was used to his wife's head strong ways, and wasn't about to deal with any female emotions unless it was from Bossee. It seemed like all the bitches he was fucking around with were in their feelings and stressing him out. All of them were texting and nagging him about money and sex. But not Bossee's ass though, because she was MIA.

"Hell nah, I'm about to go get my damn wife, fuck these hoes," Kane said out loud not caring if Torrica's crybaby ass heard him or not.

"Fuck you, Kane! Go get your wife then. She don't want you no way!" Torrica shouted.

He gathered everything of his that he'd accumulated over his time staying with Torrica and stuffed it in his duffle bag and backpack, completely ignoring a weeping Torrica. Kane had made up his mind that he was cutting everyone off to make things right with Bossee. He hurried out of the door dialing his wife's number praying he didn't have to leave yet another voicemail.

To his disappointment her voicemail picked up yet again, just as he reached his car. He was so pissed that he struggled with juggling his items and trying to hit the unlock button on the key fob. Kane threw all his bags on the ground to get his door opened. Just as he was getting everything in, his phone starting ringing.

"I knew my baby still loved me," Kane expressed as he quickly answered, letting the caller hear him.

"Huh? Um Kane. It's Nezzy, Bossee sent a text about that nigga, Poppy. We have his location, the girls and I are ready to move," Nezzy spoke in a business-like tone.

"When did you speak to Bossee last, Nez?" Kane asked, careful not to put anymore of the Bitch Gang into his marital affairs.

"She sent a text last week explaining tonight would be the day to move," Nezzy lied straight through her teeth.

She had just ended a call with her, but she wasn't about to tell his dog ass that. Bossee had been in Cancun for over a week now. She told Nezzy that she needed to clear her head, so she gathered her mother and baby girl, Kaylee, and broke out. Nezzy had to hold in her giggle on the phone because Kane sounded like a lost puppy. She didn't feel sorry for him one bit, and he had better gather himself and emotions together for tonight's mission. Nezzy wasn't friendly when she missed money, she hoped she didn't have to show Kane that.

"Okay, cool. Meet me at the mansion tonight, regular time," Kane shot back ending the call.

The entire forty-five-minute drive to his estate, he blew up his wife's phone. After a while she must have turned it off because it stopped ringing and was now going straight to her answering service. Kane threw his phone in the passenger seat. *Please God send her back to me,* he thought. Kane pulled up to his home and went inside the house praying his wife was there, even though he knew that she wasn't.

"Baby… Bossee… Keyley," Kane called out inside the empty home.

He made it up to their bedroom and checked the closets. Her stuff was still there, so he had some hope. He actually boosted his confidence that he haven't lost her. *I'll just give her a few days to clear her mind. Bossee loves me,* he thought, trying to convince himself that his wife would come home.

Seeing that it was four in the afternoon, he decided that he would take a shower and nap before the lick tonight with the girls. The nigga, Poppy who they were taking down tonight was a big score for them. Kane knew he had to be on his A game fucking with him, so he decided to push his issues with Bossee out of his mind for tonight. After taking a shower Kane relaxed downstairs while watching an old college football game that was on.

Four hours later, Kane awoke to the TV still playing old-school football highlights. It took him a few moments to gather his bearings because he didn't remember falling asleep. Remembering that there was a job with the Bitch Gang pushed him to his feet.

He still had enough time to eat, have a drink, and make it to the meeting early, so he took his time.

Thirty minutes later, Kane was seated in his office waiting for the arrival of the girls. He glanced at the cameras and saw Trendini, Torrica, and Nezzy all pulling up together. *I hope Torrica have stopped all that crying and shit, before this mission starts,* Kane mulled. Payday and meetings always happened in Kane's office so the girls made their way up the stairs to his domain. The girls filed into the room, as they made girl talk as usual.

"Well, all I know is, I'm ready to kill something. Today ain't the day," Torrica hissed, rolling her neck around.

She was still pissed at Kane from earlier, so she planned to take it out on whomever they were jacking tonight. Torrica was slowly becoming a true murderer and didn't realize it. For the first time, she was making money off something that she liked to do, *kill people.*

"Bitch, your ass is just trigga happy. You need some dick in your life so you can stop killing niggas," Nezzy jokingly implied.

"Nah, believe me I have enough dick problems now," Torrica huffed back at Nezzy as soon as they entered the room with Kane.
She made sure that she looked directly at him while saying it. Kane shot her a slit eye stare, that didn't go unnoticed by Nezzy. *Uht uht... what was that look about?* Nezzy thought to herself.

It looked to her that there was some ill feelings between Torrica and Kane, but the twins never said they had problems with him. She didn't know what the problem was, but she was going to make sure to keep an eye on everything. Bossee asked her to step up into her place while she was away. Nezzy promised her she could go get her mind right without worrying about business.

"Let's gear up and move out now. I have shit to do," Kane gruffed with much attitude as he stood up from his desk.

He was dressed in a black hoodie, black sweatpants, with black Timberland field boots. The girls all were in similar attire, but with matching black crop hoodies.

Kane stepped over to the weapon glass that held all new guns. He handed each bitch their weapon of choice, letting them choose. After they grabbed everything needed for their mission, they all piled into the black sprinter Mercedes van.

"Trendini, pull-up on Rober Lane, we will walk over to the spot from there," Kane said as he watched his surroundings. The neighborhood was upscale, quiet, and open. Trendini followed Kane's instructions without question.

"Move out bitches," Neezy spat in full gangsta mode.

As soon as the van stopped, they all hopped out quietly, making sure to not slam the doors. Kane's four-foot man soldiers followed suit closely behind them. They walked over through the side cut, up to the mansion, militantly.

"Go... go..." Kane mouthed to the girls as they approached the backdoor.

Nezzy placed the small explosive bomb near the door, they would use the sound of it as a distraction. They all separated and covered each exit from a distance.

"NOW," Kane commanded.

BOOOOOM!

The door and 12-inches around it blew off, giving the Bitch Gang access to the home. Being the trained professionals that they were, they remained in their places, with their weapons drawn. Moments after the bomb went off, two men exited from east side of the house, that Torrica had covered.

POP POP POP …

Torrica aimed and dropped both men with three shots. Two others came running through the front door which was covered by Kane's goon, Donte.

POP POP …

Donte had shot them both with expertise aim. He was really a shooter, this was all he did for a living. He went with Kane on every mission since he'd been back in Cali.

POP POP POP TAT TAT TAT …

Nezzy let off shots from her chopper. She sprayed the back of the house where she placed the bomb as warning shots. They all waited for a moment to see if anyone would return fire, but no one did. They all knew that the silence was their que to enter the house. As they all entered from different doors, they checked each room to ensure that everyone was dead.

After making sure that the coast was clear, they all made their way to the basement. Trendini had gave them the drop and information she gathered from Poppy weeks ago. It took her less than a week to get what she needed from him.

"That was too easy, shit I needed to let off some steam," Torrica complained.

Kane looked over at her and shook his head. She was irritating as fuck, but he definitely respected her gangsta.

"This where the safe is, hurry up and get the bricks," Nezzy said while moving closer in the room. She wasn't about to stand around talking when they just lit up the house. She made a mental note when she realized it of an exit close by. They all got to work, each doing their assigned task, with moving the dope and money.

When Kane opened the safe and realized it was one hundred and fifty bricks of cocaine, he almost busted a nut right there. If greed had a look, it danced on his face at the sight of all the free bands he was taking. The crew immediately realized that they had come unprepared to carry that amount of work, so Kane sent his goons to grab some more bags from the van.

"Damn, what's taking them so long?" Nezzy whispered impatiently.

Donte and Chuggs had been gone for nearly ten minutes. They had gathered everything from the safe and placed what they could in bags already.

"I'm going to find out," Kane suggested, agreeing with Nezzy.

"Well, I'm going with you," Torrica said, not waiting for a response back.

Kane knew not to dispute her coming because she was really with the shits when it came to him. They both headed upstairs, Torrica was in the lead.

Pop…

"Ouuuuuuuuch…" Torrica screeched loudly as she fell back onto Kane.

The hot bullet pierced her left leg quickly. Bullets whizzed by from what seemed like every direction.

"GET DOWN!" Kane yelped, snatching Torrica down with him.

He shot blindly at the unseen shooters in front of him. Nezzy crawled and opened the door she peeped earlier and shot it open. Trendini was shooting in the same direction Kane was.

"Sis, you are okay," Trendini said to her twin. Because she was not really sure if she was okay or not, she didn't need her to panic, they needed to figure out how they were going to escape. They made sure the house was empty before entering the basement.

Tat...Pop...Tat

"Come this way!" Nezzy screamed over the shots.

She had the door open and was peeping around it to make sure that they wouldn't be ambushed. The door was leading to the other side of backyard by the pool. Trendini ran over and helped Kane pick up Torrica. He could tell that it was probably a flesh wound so he kept telling her that she was fine. They ran behind what appeared to be a pool house for cover.

Pop pop pop pop…

Kane, Torrica, Trendini, and Nezzy let off shots at a small army of niggas as they rounded the corner.

"That's that nigga Rory," Kane grumbled when he saw Rory jump into a black Impala. He was able to see his face clearly before he hopped in the car.

"KILL THEM NIGGAS!" Torrica screamed. She was now leaning against the wall shooting at the men. She hit one of them in the neck and they watched as he fell. Rory's men grabbed him, and they all retreated to the car and van they came in.

"AYE move out now, the fucking pigs on the way," Rory yelled to his crew.

He was pissed he didn't kill Kane's ass. He followed them to this location and if he was a few moments quicker, he would've had the drop on him. He didn't care about the bitches with him, but seeing how they move, they were now on his hit list also. He had lost a soldier tonight and he wanted blood, he didn't care who's it was.

*****

A few hours later...

"Kane, seriously I almost lost my baby and I still protected you," Torrica expressed with tears in her eyes.

She was in disbelief that he was so cold hearted and still wanted her to get rid of her baby. Torrica had fallen in love with him, and all he could think of was telling Bossee what happened at the lick. They were now at the hospital in her assigned room, alone.

"Listen, I respect your gangsta, but you know how dangerous being a Bitch is. Get rid of it, T," Kane said as he turned to go into the restroom inside the hospital room.

Torrica was hurt but she knew what she had signed up for with dealing with him. So, she sucked up her tears, and got out of her feelings.

Nezzy was walking up to the room to check on Torrica when she overheard Torrica mention her baby and how she still protected Kane. She didn't know that she was pregnant, and she didn't understand why Kane would make her get rid of her baby. Shit, he could've had her do something else, like drops or count the money. If she got pregnant, Kane wouldn't tell her nothing like that, especially if it wasn't his baby. *Who is he to tell her to get rid of her baby? They fucking or something?* Nezzy thought to herself.

The more she thought about the mental notes she'd tucked away in her head she got pissed. The look at the mansion earlier that Kane gave Torrica after she said she had enough dick problems hit Nezzy's mind. *Nez, you might be tripping,* she thought while shaking her head. She walked back to the lobby to gather her mind.

"Yeah, I might be tripping, but I'm damn sure going to see if I'm not. They better not be on any slime shit, for their sakes," Neezy said as she left the hospital and hopped into her Uber. She couldn't even go see Torrica with the shit on her mind, so we went home and calmed her nerves from the day.

CHAPTER FOURTEEN

Cancun...

Bossee sat in the sand on a beach towel while sitting next to her mother. They were watching her daughter build a sand castle a few feet away from them while they sipped margaritas. Bossee was finally starting to feel refreshed. She felt like she had to up and leave because she needed some space. Not only was she cleansing from Kane, she was cleansing from Rory as well. After her one night with him at the Laker game, she found herself in his arms every night. They hadn't fucked since their moment in the box but being with him felt so right but she knew it was wrong.

Bossee was still married to Kane and he still had that tug on her heart. She was starting to miss Kane as the days went by and even started feeling like maybe they could fix things. They were in business together and she didn't want to be beefing with him while they were getting money. Rory was a cool guy, but he wasn't Kane and she didn't know the real him. She knew him from high school and the little that he showed her when they were together, and that was it.

After finding out he was a drug dealer, it really made her think. She figured he was a street nigga like Kane and probably had a bunch of bitches just like Kane. He came in her life at a time when she was hurt, and she appreciated the love he showed her. But she knew it was time to go home and face her truth about Kane.

"So, are you going to finally tell me why we snuck to Cancun and ain't tell nobody, Allaysia?" her mother asked, snapping her out her thoughts.
Bossee sighed and looked over at her mother.

She looked like a celebrity in her one-piece silver bathing suit and silver circle sunglasses covering her green eyes, like her daughter. Her mother was fifty-five years old, but didn't look a day over thirty-five. People always thought her mother was her big sister because they looked so much alike. She gazed at her mother with sad eyes because she knew it was time to tell her the truth.

"Ma, Kane is cheating on me and has been for a long time."

Her mother shook her head.

"Well, what you gonna do?" She took off her shades and gazed at Bossee.

That was the first time she saw the pain in her eyes.

"I wanted to leave his ass, I even found me a new nigga. But as I got closer to my new dude, I felt like it was wrong. So, I'm leaving here and going home to Kane."

She gazed over at her daughter, "oh hell no, I say leave his ass. Once a cheater, always a cheater. I know you are thinking of Keyley, but you need to think of yourself as well."

Bossee knew her mother was right, but she wanted to give Kane another chance. He was all she really knew and chasing her bag with him was something she didn't want to give up.

"He got one more time mama, I promise."

"Well if he cut up again, show his ass who's boss."

Bossee laughed, "I hear you mama."

The sun was going down, so they packed up and headed back to their villa that was located on the beach. When they got back, they started packing to go home the following morning. Bossee decided to turn on her phone. As soon as she turned it on, she had so many messages from Kane and the girls. The only person knew she was gone was Nezzy. She skimmed through all of Kane's sad messages and figured she would just talk to him when she got home. She knew he had to be drowning in misery by now so she knew he would be powered down when she got home. Only then, could they have a civilized conversation.

While still scrolling, she ran into a text from Rory.

Rory: I miss you Miss Lady, you just disappeared on me. Text me back.

She sat there gazing at his message. A long tear fell from her left eye. She couldn't deny that she had caught feelings for Rory. Everything about him was perfect, but that wasn't her man. She was not married to him. However, she felt she owed him the truth and decided to tell him she was going to work things out with her husband.

Bossee: I went on vacation. I'll get with you in a few days…

This shit better work out with Kane because if it doesn't, I'm killing his ass and moving on with Rory, was her last thought before she turned off her phone again...

*****

Bossee and her mom pulled up to her home in an Uber. Bossee couldn't wait to dump her bags and get some sleep. She had been baking in the sun for a week. Now it was time for her to relax at home and get rid of her jet lag. Their Uber driver pulled into Bossee's long driveway and parked behind a brand-new cocaine white Porsche truck. It was beautiful with a red bow wrapped around it. Bossee's heart sank as her mother sat next to her and shook her head.

Her mother knew exactly what was going on, but she decided to stay out her daughter business.

"You want me to take Keyley with me and you go work things out?" her mom asked. Although she felt like her decision was wrong, she was going to support her decisions.

"You wanna go with Nana?" Bossee asked Keyley, and she shook her head yes.
She was tired as well and didn't care whose house she was going to.

"I'll pick her up later or in the morning," Bossee opened the door and stepped out.

After she carried her things to the door, she kissed Keyley and her mother goodbye.

Bossee left her bags in her foyer and then started walking towards her living room.

"Kane, babbbyyyy, where arreeee youuu?" she sang as her heels clicked the marble floor. The house was quiet until she heard her TV in the living room playing low. She walked into the living room and spotted Kane slouching on the couch with the remote and a bottle of Patron in his hand. She looked at his appearance and she had never seen him looking so depressed and underdressed.

His five o'clock shadow beard looked like he hadn't shaved in weeks. Kane was always well kept even lounging around the house, but not in this moment. He had a lot on his mind, and his appearance was the last thing on his mind.

"Where the fuck you been, Allaysia? I been fucking blowing you up and you walk in here like ain't shit going on," he said in a low roar.

"I went to Cancun with my mom and Keyley. I needed to get away without anybody knowing."

"You should have told me. I was trying to make shit up with you because I know I been doing some fucked up shit, and ya ass wasn't even here."

"I know, I saw the truck out front. I love it. And I came home to work shit out with you too. I love you Kane, but you gotta stop cheating on me and doing me dirty," she flopped on the couch next to him.

He looked like he needed a hug, so she wrapped her arms around him.

"I ain't seen my fuckin' daughter, Bossee. You been doing too much too. You ain't been home in a month damn near. I been out here with the girls getting this money, and Torrica in the hospital."

Bossee was caught off guard with what he had just said about Torrica.

"Torrica's in the hospital?" – She took her arms from around him. – "What happened to her?"

"We was bussin a lick and she got hit. She good, but they want to keep her for a few days."

"Damn, I'll go visit her later. But right now, we need to fix us. Don't make this shit about me, it all happened because you can't keep ya dick in ya pants. I do everything a wife is supposed to do, and you still run around on me. It's stupid, Kane. We're not teenagers anymore. You need to grow up and respect me as your wife."

"I'm sorry, Bossee."

He put his head down in shame. Kane was doing more than Bossee could imagine that's why he felt so fucked up. He had gotten her cousin pregnant and now he was caught all in her web. He had changed his number on his other females, but he kept running back to Torrica, especially since Bossee had disappeared on him.

"Let's start over babe," Bossee whispered.

She meant every word she said to her husband. She wanted them to go back to loving each other.

The sexual tension between the two heightened, so Kane pulled his wife up with him as he stood. He placed little kisses, starting from her forehead and ended on her sexy lips. Bossee kissed on Kane while throwing her arms around his waist. Kane was so much taller than she was, so he had to bend down to kiss her. Kane lifted the maxi dress Bossee wore over her head and found nothing underneath.

"Damn, B, your body is sexy as fuck," Kane moaned as he stepped a couple steps back to admire her.

Not wasting anymore time gazing at her, he guided her to the couch, laying her on her back. Kane lifted both of her legs up and dove in face first. No matter how many bitches he cheated with, he never ate anyone else's pussy. Her nectar was sweet and didn't have a smell at all. Kane rolled his lips from side to side on her pearl.

"Shhhhhhh…Kaneeee," Bossee groaned loudly.

It had been so long since the last time her husband touched her, she was ready to explode.

Bossee thrusted her hips in the opposite direction of his lips and tongue. Kane knew she was close to her peak, so he flicked his tongue quickly, then drove it inside of her pussy. The pressure caused Bossee to squirt her juice all over Kane's face.

"Damn, baby you missed daddy huh," he yelped as he got up and removed his briefs.

Bossee wasted no time getting on all fours with her back arched. Kane placed one of his feet on the couch to get a better grip. Taking his large hands, he grabbed her ass and pushed his huge dick inside of a dripping wet Bossee.

"Awww baby. Thank you for not giving my pussy up," Kane yelled out because she felt exactly like how he left her last time they fucked.

Bossee almost dried up as soon as he said it, but she kept cool and twerked on his dick. *Damn, I can't believe I fucked Rory,* Bossee thought to herself. She quickly forgot her thought as Kane began to punish her kitty. He was hitting her g-spot and she was about to bust off again.

"Awe, babeee! I swear I will never cheat on you again," Kane huffed as he continued to pump in and out of Bossee.

"Prom..ise… meeee," Bossee huffed back.
Kane flipped her around and started slow stroking like his life depended on it.

"I promise, baby," Kane uttered.

"Pick me up nigga," Bossee demanded, changing the tune of their love making.
Kane did as he was told without missing a stroke. They fucked each throughout the house for hours. They ended in their bedroom naked on the floor.

"Bossee, I meant everything I said, I'm sorry," Kane said to his half sleeping wife.
She was laying on his chest as he rubbed her back.

"Okay, baby," was all she said back as they drifted off into dreamland.

Bossee woke up to nightfall. She was still laid on the floor with Kane. She looked over at him, he was laying on his back with his arm covering his face, naked. A sense of irritation crossed her mind as she gazed at him. She was in a good mood when she came home, confident about what she had with Kane. But her little nap had her mind somewhere else. *I forgave this nigga,* she thought to herself as she shook her head, looking at him in disgust. The many bodies he had on him from cheating left her stomach turning. *He ain't gonna change,* she thought again. Bossee kicked him slightly in the side, trying to wake him up.

"Oh shit, it's time to go?" he jumped up and said.

Bossee chuckled, "go where Kane?" she asked.

"I don't know, I'm trippin. What time is it?" he asked in a confused tone as he stood up to his feet.

Bossee looked on their nightstand at the time.

"It's only 7:30. You wanna go with me to see Torrica?" she asked.

She flicked on every light in the room. Kane frowned as he rubbed his eyes.

"Nah, I'm sick of seeing her and the other girls. I'm about to head out to my barber before he close and then I'ma go do some pickups."

"Alright. I'll see you later then. Don't stay out all night either. We supposed to be getting our shit right."

"I know Bossee…" he said as he disappeared into the bathroom.

Bossee walked into her closet and picked out a cute sweat suit.

The weather was funny in Cali since it was late winter, so she had to dress for the rain. She walked to her daughter's room and decided to shower in her bathroom. She showered and got dress. Within minutes, she was out the door in her brand-new Porsche truck. The key was already in the passenger waiting for her. She called Nezzy while she was on her way and got the rundown on what happened.

"Girl, y'all need to cool down with the violence before somebody dies," Bossee expressed as she got on the freeway with Nezzy on speaker.

"Look, niggas was shooting at us. We went and did what we did and ran into trouble. Big bad Torrica just had to take her ass with Kane to see what was going on and got hit. But she good, she's at Cedars. It was a flesh wound but they are keeping her for some shit. You will find out when you get there," Nezzy expressed.

"Alright, I'm pulling up in ten minutes. You wanna meet up for dinner in like an hour or so?"

"Yeah, I'm bored as fuck so meet me at Fridays. Let's do some regular dining."

"Alright I'll call you."

Ten minutes later, Bossee pulled into the hospital's parking lot. She walked in and went to the information desk and got a badge. She took the elevator to the third floor and got off. When she got off, she realized that she was in the psych ward. *Oh lawd, what this bitch den did?* Bossee thought to herself when she walked the halls looking for Torrica's room.

Bossee knew there was something wrong with her cousin since they were little. For as long as she could remember, Torrica's mom had her in and out of counselling because she was so violent and rebeliant. Bossee thought about it all when she first put her cousins on, but figured since she had been in the game for a few years that she could handle it. Now her gut was telling her, she wasn't fit.

Bossee snapped out her thoughts when she walked in front of Torrica's door. The door was cracked so she pushed it open. She walked in the dark room and heard crying coming from Torrica's bed. Bossee walked over to her and found Torrica in a fetal position with the cover over her head. A weary feeling came over Bossee when she laid eyes on Torrica. She didn't look like the that Torrica she knew. Her skin was pale, and she had dark circles around her eyes. Her usually big gray eyes were low and red. Bossee sighed.

"T, you okay? What's going on? Why you in the ward?" Bossee asked in a low tone as she stood over her bed.

Torrica turned around and looked at Bossee. She didn't say a word to her, she just started crying. Bossee sat there staring at her. She had no idea what was going on and it was a little too awkward for her.

"I'm fucked up, Allaysia!" she shouted. Bossee looked at the door and saw that it was open. She didn't want doctors coming in, so she closed it and then walked over to Torrica.

"T, you know your mental ain't right, so the shit you be doing is too much. If hitting these licks are too much, get out."

"I've killed so many people, I got so much blood on my hands, and I've done everyone wrong that's showed me any good. Now I'm fucking pregnant by a nigga that don't want me, and he wants me to get rid of it. It's my baby, I should be able to keep it," she continued to cry. Torrica had been on seventy-two hours hold because she snapped when Kane left her alone.

The doctors knew something was wrong with her, so they kept her instead of releasing her.

"And, you're right. But do you think you can run the streets with a baby?"

"You do it, why can't I?" Torrica wept.

"You can't be me, T. I've told you this for years. Stop trying to chase after what I be doing. The shit I do, I know I shouldn't be doing with a daughter, but I do because that shit is in me. I don't need another me running around here with a baby, setting niggas up. Be better than me. Kids can wait, get this money," Bossee preached.

"I don't understand why I can't be normal like you and my sister. I've had this demon inside of me since I was a kid. Doing bad shit and being punished for it. Story of my life."

Bossee knew she wasn't going to ever get her cousin to understand anything, so she just listened to her ramble on. She knew she was sick and needed help outside of her.

"Look, Torrica... I know we don't see eye to eye, but you know I got your back. You've always been loyal to me, so whatever you need, let me know. I'll talk to the nurses and see about getting you out of here. You can stay at the trap mansion and get your mind right. You know we got seven rooms available in that bitch," Bossee said as she handed her a box of Kleenex.

"Thank you… I look fucked up, huh? I snatched off my wig and the nurse threw it away," she shook her head.

Bossee laughed, "I'll get somebody to come up here and hook you up if they don't release you before then."

"Okay, my nurse should be in here with my meds and Trendini brought me food, so I'm good."

"Alright, you hang in there, girl."

Bossee walked out of the room. She went into deep thought as she made her way down the hall and outside to her truck. Torrica was a mess and she knew she had to pull her from the clique. It wasn't healthy so she decided to talk to Kane about pulling her and replacing her...

CHAPTER FIFTEEN

Three days later...

Rory sat in the driver seat of his brand-new black on black dodge Challenger, in deep thought. He almost had Kane in his hands, but it was too much going on. All he saw was a bunch of females shooting, so he shot as much as he could and got on with his men. When he got word of Kane's next move, he had to try his luck. He knew it was a bad to move in on him while Kane was on a mission, but he didn't give a fuck, he wanted him dead. *I'ma catch his silly ass, watch...* he thought.

Rory looked out the window and watched the rain fall. It was three in the afternoon and he was waiting for Allaysia to pull up in front of his building. She said she was on the move and only had a few minutes to spend with him, so he agreed to meet her outside. At that moment, Rory saw a white on white Porsche truck pull in front of him. He watched the truck parallel park like a pro and then he saw Bossee step out with her huge brown Fendi umbrella. She was wearing a tight knitted brown turtleneck dress that stopped at her thighs with a pair of suede brown stiletto boots.

"Damn, this woman stay fly," Rory said out loud as he watched her strut to his passenger side. Rory hit the locks. Bossee stepped in after she closed her umbrella.

"You can toss that big muthafucka in the back," Rory said, referring to her umbrella. She sat her umbrella on the back floor.

"It's raining cats and dogs in Cali. This is why I left South Carolina," Bossee said as she reached over and embraced Rory.

"Oh, you lived in S.C?" he asked with his eyebrow raised.

For some reason hearing South Carolina reminded him of Kane. He knew that was where the nigga was from.

"For a lil bit… But what's up with you? You are looking fly in your glasses and tie," Bossee smiled while checking out his appearance.

She then looked down at his Versace loafers, they were black and gold.

"Court for my bro earlier. But where you been? A nigga was missing you."

"I missed you too, but I had to get away. Shit is crazy right now in my life," she sighed and looked down at her ring finger.

She was back wearing her wedding band because Kane wouldn't let her leave without it now. Rory glanced at her finger again. *She back with her nigga,* he thought to himself. *Well if they was back on for real, she wouldn't be here with me,"* he thought again, but he didn't say anything.

When it came to her and her marriage, he always let her speak first.

"I hear you. But I think I got something that will cheer you up."

He reached into his center console and pulled out a rose gold watch box. He handed it to Bossee. She gazed at the box and it said *Rolex*.

"You didn't have too, Rory," she said as she gazed at the box.

Her heart was thumping because she knew it was some fly shit inside the box.

"I did. I noticed your drip, so I wanted to add to it. Open it," he smiled.

He was anxious to see her reaction. Bossee opened the box and laid her eyes on an iced out rose gold Rolex watch.

The diamonds damn near blinded her as she gazed at it. She sighed, not giving the smile that he was waiting on. Instead, she closed the box.

"I can't accept this gift Rory. It's too much," she handed him the box.

"What chu mean?" he asked in confusion.

He wasn't expecting to be turned down.

"I'm not your girl, I'm married, and I'm trying to work things out with him."

He frowned, "that ain't what it's been looking like, Allaysia. You sitting here with me, it's evident you ain't happy."

"You don't know my story, Rory," – she paused because she heard her phone buzzing in her purse by her foot. – "Hold up," she put her finger up. Rory was so agitated that he could've gotten out his own car and walked in the rain. He felt like Allaysia was toying with his heart and he was done with it.

"Aye, you gotta get out my shit. You are being really disrespectful and ion like that," Rory roared at her as he gazed at her looking through her phone.

"It's not even like that."

That's when he noticed a long tear fall from her eyes. He didn't know what was going on, but he regretted yelling at her. Bossee, however, couldn't believe what she was seeing. It was a video from Nezzy of Kane and Torrica coming out of Planned Parenthood. He had his arm around her, and she looked like she was crying.

"Look at this," Bossee passed her phone to Rory.

He gazed at it and then took it in his hands. When he saw that it was Kane and the same bitch that he knew he had shot, rage came across his dome.

"Aye yo, what the fuck is this? That's that country nigga that been running up in my spots," Rory said as he gazed at the phone with his face balled up with anger.

"You trying to set me up?" he discreetly reached under his seat for his .38 revolver and pointed it at Bossee.

She threw her hands up in defense, she was not expecting him to do that.

"Woah, my nigga chill. I'm not trying to set you up, I'm not that kind of bitch. That is my husband and that's my first cousin. They fuckin behind my back and my best friend just showed me this video."

"Well how the fuck you know I know this nigga?" he asked with his gun still pointed at Bossee.

"Look, I know a lot. The operation he runs, I'm the mastermind behind it but I didn't know he was going to be hitting niggas like he is. I also didn't know he was fucking my cousin and got her pregnant until now. So, what the fuck you wanna do? You wanna help me ride this shit out or you gonna shoot me. I know where your worst enemy is, Rory, you need me."

"I don't need shit from you, bitch, but for you to get the fuck out my whip. I'm done with your conniving ass," he snarled at her.

"Please, Rory. Don't do this, now is not the time. The only reason I know you had ties with him was because I saw your number in his phone. I didn't say anything because I didn't know what was going on. But, I can help you baby," she said in a low tone that touched Rory's heart.

He didn't want to kill her, and he had heard everything that she had said but his ego was running his mind at that moment.

"You fucking up my mental right now, Allaysia. What the fuck!"

"I'm sorry Rory. I swear, I like you more than I should, but I knew being married and being with you wasn't right. You are right, I'm not happy, but I be trying to make shit right for my daughter. I been with this nigga for six years, he's all I know. I didn't know he was beefing with you, and I promise I don't have shit to do with anything he's ever did to you." Rory sighed as he watched the tears from her eyes fall. She was tugging at his heart. He was past the *like* stage with Allaysia, he was in love. But he never told her for this very reason, *he didn't know the real her.*

He sat his gun in his lap and handed her the phone.

"So, what you wanna do? That nigga fuckin' your cousin and he killed my nephews. I want to body that nigga, I don't care if he your child's father. I want that niggas head," he roared.

"Follow me to my best friend house. Trust me, me and my girl got you. We know this nigga like a book."

She grabbed her umbrella from his back seat and then reached into her large Louis Vuitton handbag for her piece. She flashed her gun at Rory.

"And from here on out, they call me Bossee, and I tote guns just like you. Pull a gun out on me again and you won't make it, playboy."

Rory watched her step out his car and walk to her truck with her gun to her side while holding her umbrella.

"Damn, that's a bad bitch right there," he uttered as he started up his car and trailed behind her to the southside of L.A in the rain.

*****

Earlier...

Nezzy sat in the parking lot of planned parenthood waiting on Torrica to pull up. She had just spoken with her and she said that she was on her way to get the abortion that she had kept telling her about. Nezzy made sure she pulled up first and parked in the back of the parking lot so that she could lurk. She was dying to know who Torrica's baby daddy was. And she knew if she was going to the clinic the nigga was going to be there to make sure that she did it. Nezzy lit her blunt as she waited for Torrica to pull-up.

Ten minutes of waiting she saw Kane's black on black Benz that he never drove anymore pull into a parking space near the back, not far from her. Nezzy face turned bright red, and she knew steam was coming from her ears.

"Torrica better not be in this car because I swear I'm going to beat her assss," Nezzy said out loud to herself.

As soon as the words left her mouth, Torrica hopped out of the passenger seat, and slammed the door. Nezzy grabbed her cellphone and opened her

Snapchat app. She secretly recorded the encounter playing out before her eyes.

"I bet if my cousin was the one pregnant, you wouldn't make her kill her baby. I fucking hate YOU," Torrica screamed, making a scene.

"Bitch, nobody told you to get pregnant. That's what's wrong with bitches these days, always worried about the wrong shit. You knew I was married to your fucking cousin," Kane's voice boomed loudly as he hopped out of the car.

He snatched her up by her arm and literally dragged her while walking towards the entrance.

"FUCK YOU, KANE," Torrica cried out as Nezzy ended the recording.

Nezzy wanted to get out the car and shoot them both, but she calmed herself. She immediately went to Bossee's name in her Snapchat contacts and sent her the video. She sent a message with it.

I'm still here, tell me if you want me to step now or not.

Bossee opened the message immediately. Nezzy knew this was going to break her friend's heart and it made her even more mad. She waited for her to respond but she never did.

"SHIT," Nezzy spat out loud hitting her steering wheel.

She knew this wasn't her business so she would only move how Bossee said to. The thing about Nezzy was once she was mad, she had to do something.

A smile formed on her face when she remembered she had a knife with her. She quickly dug it out of her purse and hopped out the car. Nezzy went to Kane's car and sliced each tire. She made sure that they all went flat. *Now, bitch ass nigga,* she thought as she pulled off. She called Bossee but she didn't answer. A text came through from her immediately.

Bossee Bae: Meet me at your house

Bet! Was all Nezzy replied as she hit the gas pedal, speeding to her friend's side.

CHAPTER SIXTEEN

A couple hours later…

Bossee sat behind the wheel of her truck crying her eyes out. She was sitting in front of Nezzy's apartment building with Rory parked directly behind her. Her heart was breaking by the minute and it was hard for her to control her feelings. She had dealt with Kane's infidelities with random bitches, but for him to fuck her first cousin and get her pregnant had her ready to body his ass.

She was so caught up in the money and her own life, she didn't see the shit happening right in her face. She thought back to all the times she was in the same room with them and they acted as though shit was cool, all while they were fucking. She thought Kane was better than he showed her. She thought he was better than her ex, but he wasn't. She hit her steering wheel causing her horn to honk.

"Shit," she said as she looked in her rearview and saw Rory's door open.

She reached into her bag and pulled out some tissue to wipe her face. She pulled down her visor and looked at her reflection. Her mascara was smearing.

Rory knocked her on window as she was finishing up her makeup.

"What's good? you okay in here?" he asked with a concerned look on his face.

"Yeah I'm good. I was calling my cousin to come over and accidently hit the horn."

He gazed into her eyes and could tell that she had been crying.

"You ain't gotta cry, lil mama. This shit going to be over soon," he said in a sincere tone.

"I know, the shit is just fucked up and unexpected, ya know?" she shrugged her shoulders.

"Yeah I feel you. Dude a clown…."

Bossee's phone vibrated in her lap. It was Trendini saying that she was on her way to Nezzy's.

Bossee sent her a text telling her that they needed to have an important meeting.

"I'm about to get out. Wait for me in front of that gate."

Rory walked off and Bossee continued to fix her face. A couple minutes later, she was stepping out, stomping in a huge puddle messing up her boots.

"Shit, today just ain't my day."

She stepped on the curb and met Rory at the gate. She reached in her bag and got out the keycard to the front of Nezzy's building. Bossee had full access to Nezzy's apartment. She even had her house key. Bossee followed the bass of the trap music she heard playing loud throughout the building.

She knew it was Nezzy, being hood in a well put together building.

"That's my BFF playing that music. When you meet her you gonna trip, she's Spanish and Black but ratchet as hell. She's cool tho' and she gangsta as fuck. You're going to like her." Bossee was giving him a heads up on Nezzy because she knew that she was a handful.

Rory chuckled, “I’m sure I’ll be fine, thanks for letting me know tho’.”

Bossee used her key and opened Nezzy’s door. They stepped into her apartment and it was decked out.

She had white leather couches and a huge lion rug that stretched out on her living room floor. She had her black lights going and she had lavender oil burning with Kush smoke in the air. Rory glanced at her glass coffee table and saw all her guns, kilos, and money scattered on the table. *Yeah, this bitch official,* Rory thought as he looked around.

“Bossee Bitch! What the fuck is up! Uth uth, who is this fine ass nigga! You ain’t tell me you was bringing him!” – Nezzy said loudly as she eyed Rory. – “Y’all want a drink?” she asked as she walked towards her coffee table and picked up a bottle of champagne.

Rory couldn’t help but to stare at her huge ass.

Although he knew it was fake, the shit was fat.

"Yes, we do. And, this is my nigga… his name is Rory," she smirked at him and he nodded.

"Okay bitch! I see you." Neezy was blushing like it was her getting a new man.

Bossee slid her ring off her finger and dropped it in Nezzy's champagne bottle.

"Bitch! you serious huh, well fuck that nigga! He slimy as fuck and I'm ready for whatever you got planned."

Nezzy took her Moet Rose to the head, even with the ring in it.

"Yeah, and with that, I want to talk about a few things before Trendini gets here. Right now, you and Rory are the only ones I trust. I trust Trendini, but with her sister tied in this shit, I know she's going to side with her," Bossee stated as she walked over to the couch with Rory.

Nezzy grabbed two glasses from her bar and passed one to Rory and Bossee. They both helped themselves to her champagne while Nezzy grabbed her weed tray to roll a blunt.

"Alright sis, spill it."

"You been working heavy with Kane lately so I'm sure you know his beef. This is Rory, he's been beefing with Kane. He's the one that shot Torrica."

Rory cut his eyes over to Bossee, but before he spoke up, Nezzy began to talk.

"Rory? Nah, he ain't never said anything to me about him. Must be that mission him and Torrica was on. But what the fuck, what's all this about then? You throwing me off babe," Nezzy expressed in a confused tone.

"I wasn't expecting you to say all that, but since it's out there, I don't know who this nigga is, to be honest. He been breaking in my spots, killing my fam, and looking for me to get put on his team. I told him I was good, and the nigga has been a thorn in my ass ever since. I shot at the nigga when he was on a lick at somebody else's crib. Now I'm finding out this nigga is married to her," – he pointed at Bossee – "All I know is, I want this nigga out of here, bad," Rory took his cup of champagne to the head. The wrinkles that were forming in his forehead let Nezzy know that he was not playing.

"Wow, okay so what's next? I want this nigga head too and the rest of the money he owes me. I wasn't going to say nothing to see if my shit was short this next time but fuck it now!" Nezzy sparked her blunt.

As soon as the Kush hit her lungs she started choking.

"First things first, we're moving all his work to another location tomorrow night, and I'm finna drain our account and put it in my personal one tonight. Don't worry 'bout that money he owes you, I'ma get that too you A.S.A.P."

"Well, I slashed that nigga tires and he had a tow truck pick him and Torrica pitiful ass up. I followed them before I came home. After he switched cars, they headed to some low budget hotel by the airport."

"Wow, this nigga fucking with her like that? We gonna get both they asses," Bossee said as she shook her head.

At that moment, they heard a knock at Nezzy's door. They knew it was Trendini so Nezzy opened the door before looking. When Trendini walked in, the room was weary. Rory looked at her and frowned. *Is this the cousin, the bitch that's fuckin' her husband?* he thought to himself as he eyed her. She looked just like the girl he had shot.

"Come on in, Trendini! We got some shit to lay on you and we need answers," Neezy said as she followed behind Trendini to the couch.
She flopped on the loveseat and Nezzy sat next to her.

"What's up? What happened? It's my twin, huh?"

"Oh yes, this has everything to do with Torrica," Bossee stood up.

"I'ma step outside and let y'all talk I need to make a few calls," Rory said, not wanting to be in the middle of female drama.

After Rory left out, the conversation started.

"You knew Torrica was fucking Kane and got pregnant by him?" Bossee asked.

Trendini looked at Bossee with shock written all over her face. She truly didn't know and had thought Torrica had let that situation go.

"I swear to God I didn't know that. But I'ma be honest, I did know she was crushing on him a couple months back and I told her to back off for the sake of you and the business, and she said okay."

"Well, I'm finna hurt this bitch and some shit about to happen to this grimy nigga Kane. So, is you rocking with us or what?" Bossee barked as Nezzy looked on, letting Bossee take the stage.

Trendini was so upset at her sister, but she couldn't believe Bossee was going to try and hurt her twin. She knew her sister was wrong, but she couldn't ride on Torrica for it. They shared the same womb and she loved her sister even with all her flaws.

"Nah, I can't even do it, cuzzo. I'll ride with you on Kane but not my sis."

"Well I'm going to drag your punk ass sister, family or not. The bitch ain't that fucking crazy to not mess with my man, my husband. I don't give a fuck if he came at her first or vice versa, they both crossed me. So, listen to me now, Trendini, if you don't wake up with a twin, don't come for me. Because I'll do you worse than I do her," Bossee could feel her rage building up and Trendini didn't want any smoke with her cousin.

Trendini stood up and grabbed her handbag.

"Do what you gotta do, but I ain't in it." – She started walking to the door. – "I love you Bossee, but I can't do this shit nomo. I'm out the business, y'all can do what you want with Kane..."

Nezzy followed behind Trendini.

"Don't be out the business Trendini, just think about it. I'll speak for Bossee, you ain't gotta ride on your twin but help us get that nigga Kane. Remember, he owes you money too and he been cutting your sis a fat check because she been sucking his dick for that bag. You been working."

Trendini gazed at her and Bossee, "I'll think about it…"

She headed for the door. After the door slammed Nezzy and Bossee sighed.

"Damn, man this shit is fucked up. This nigga is tearing us apart. I don't want to see Trendini go, that's my girl. And I'm so pissed at Torrica. How could she do this?"

Neezy relit her blunt. Her nerves were so bad from the drama.

"I know, but fuck them, we will worry about sisterhood later. But right now, I'ma come up with a plan for Kane and Torrica's bitch asses, so sit tight until I call you."

Bossee downed her champagne and sat the cup on the table.

"I'ma go chill out with Rory and work this plan out. More than likely we finna pop up on Kane and Torrica. Surprise they dirty ass."

Bossee headed for the door.

"Alright boo, I'll be waiting. I love you and be safe, okay?"

Nezzy and Bossee hugged. When Bossee made it to the front of the building she spotted Rory pacing back and forth on the phone while smoking his blunt. She walked over to him and he dismissed his call.

"Is everything straightened out? I saw ol girl leave mad as fuck."

"She will be aight. But I'm ready to get out here, I need to relax my mind."

Bossee walked up to her truck and opened the door. She got in and sat in her driver seat.

"Alright, you want me to follow you home and make sure you good?" he asked as he passed her the blunt.

"Yeah, I need to get some clothes because actually I was thinking I can go to your place and make shit up to you. You know, cooookk…. fuccckkkk… and you give me my watch back," she smirked as she sized him with her eyes sexually.

With everything going on with Kane, she couldn't wait to jump Rory's bone.

Rory chuckled.

"Yeah, we can do that and yeah you can have your watch. I also want to apologize for disrespecting you earlier and pulling my burner out on you. A nigga just got feelings for you, so I can't lie I was hurtin'," he put his head down.

That was the first time Rory ever found himself coming off as vulnerable.

"I have feelings for you too, Rory. So, after all of this I want to know if we can start fresh like I was never married?"

"Of course. Just know I'll never be like your bitch ass husband. I don't conduct business like him and I damn sure would never treat a beautiful woman like you the way he did. I got you, no matter what," he kissed her lips.

"I hear you Rory. It's cold, let's head to your place and we can talk more there."

Rory closed her door and then headed to his car. He was happy with the way things were going. Only thing, Kane was still alive and he wasn't going to be able to get good sleep until he was dead. *I'm finna finally get this nigga,* Rory thought as he drove off following Bossee to her house.

*****

After following Bossee to her home for clothes, and then to the grocery store so she could pick up a few things for their dinner, they headed to his apartment. It had started pouring down raining again, so they quickly went inside. Bossee showered and put on something comfortable. Rory turned on some oldies and made them drinks and rolled a few blunts. It felt good for him to have Bossee back in his presence and this time they were official.

"Okay, I see you in here throwing down," Rory said when he walked into the kitchen and passed Bossee a glass of D'usse on ice, the way she liked it.

"I do a lil something," she said with a smirk as she flipped their steaks.

She took a sip of her drink and then sat it on the counter.

"I love me a woman that can throw down. I can get used to this, keep a nigga home," he smiled.

"I hope so."

Rory gazed at her and thought back to what she spoke on when they were at Nezzy's crib. He couldn't believe a woman like her was behind a drug operation. A gangster's wife he could see because she definitely looked good on his arm. But to run an operation was insane to him.

"How long you been in the game?" Rory asked.

"I've been in the drug business all my life. It's been in my family for generations. I tried to stay in school through college, but the streets were bringing in way more than school."

Rory nodded.

"So, you know where all that nigga Kane shit is, huh?" Rory asked nonchalantly as he sipped his drink.

"Yup, he got a warehouse at the bottom of his trap spot. I have full access to it, and we have a joint account with 2 mil in it. I'ma drain that bitch, and I'm wondering if you are willing to take all the dope and sell it for me with Nezzy. I'll run you your cut."

"Aight, bet."

Thirty minutes later, dinner was done. Bossee and Rory threw down in his living room while watching the movie *Friday*. With so much going on around them, they just wanted to relax for the night and watch funny movies. After they ate, Bossee washed up all the dishes and they started on another drink and a movie. They sat taking shots of cognac. By this time they were on *Friday after Next*. Bossee laid her head on his chest and started running her hand down his chest in his wife beater.

Her touch alone had Rory turned on. However, he didn't move, he wanted to see what her next move was. She continued to rub his chest until she made her way down to his sweats. She reached her hands inside of his boxers and started stroking his manhood to an erection.

"Mmm, damn, that feels good babe," Rory spoke in a low seductive tone.

Bossee felt his precum thru her fingers so she pulled out his stick and took him to the back of her throat. Rory was surprised she was taking it there. They hadn't even had sex since their moment in the skybox.

"Shit, Bossee, suck that shit," Rory uttered as he looked down at her deepthroat his ten inches. He had never had a woman that could take him to the back of their throat successfully. That alone had him wanting to marry her.

Bossee was enjoying sucking the soul out of his body. It had been so long since she went down on a guy. It had been almost a year since she sucked

Kane's dick because she didn't trust him. So, sucking on Rory freely had her feeling good. She was a woman that was into pleasing her man. She wasn't ashamed of her love for sex. But once she felt betrayed by Kane, she stripped him from a lot of a man's needs.

Rory was mind blown by her head game so much that he was ready to nut after a few minutes.

"Stand up and take off your clothes, I wanna see that body," Rory uttered to her.

Bossee stood in front of Rory and pulled her sweats to her ankles along with her panties. As she was slipping off her top, Rory dove face first into her nectar. Bossee moaned out when his tongue found her clit.

"Yes, Rory," – she moaned – "right there."

Bossee put her hand on top of his head and rubbed his waves while he sent her into pure ecstasy.

She thought it was so ironic that she was with her high school crush after all these years. To her, he wasn't just the next drug dealer that scored her, he was her dream man that she had always wanted. That was one of the reasons why she let him in her world so easily. Rory lifted her up and sat her on his face. He rested his head back on the couch and let Bossee go to work on his tongue. She was in her zone as she rode his face, cumming back to back.

She looked over her shoulder and saw that he was rock hard. She slid off his face and slid down on his dick. She wasn't worried about a condom this time, she wanted to feel all of him.

Before she got in the position to ride him, he slipped his arm behind her and laid her on the couch.

"I'm fuckin' you this time," he smirked and slid inside of her.

"Shiiiit, Rory," she cooed as he gave her slow deep strokes.

He kissed all on her neck and then made his way to her lips. He bit her bottom lip gently as he smirked and dug inside of her deeper.

"Fuccckkk," she exclaimed as she arched her back in ecstasy.

Rory was doing something to her body that she had never felt before. He put her legs almost to her shoulders and sped up his pace.

The sound of her juices smacking on his pelvis had him completely turned on. Rory was totally in his zone. Bossee felt like she was in heaven as she took each one of his strokes. She was so tight, yet she didn't squirm from his strokes.

"Yes, Rory, fuck meee," Bossee cried out.

She reached up and bit his lip. Rory smirked and wiped sweat from his forehead, he knew he was giving her the business.

"Let's take this to my room, I need space," Rory said as he stood up and looked at Bossee laying in a daze as she played with her nipples.

He grabbed her hand and made her stand up. He looked at the wet spot on his couch and shook his head. Luckily his couch was stain proof. He led her to the bedroom and turned on the light.

"Bend that ass over," Rory smacked her ass and Bossee fell onto the bed laughing.

"Somebody is aggressive in bed, I like that," Bossee bit down on her bottom lip as she got into position.

Rory wasted no time sliding his rod back inside of his lady. He started off slowly but quickly sped up as his dick became hard as cement. Bossee was turning him on more and more with her pretty fuck faces and moans. She was throwing her ass back in a circle, roughly. Rory wanted her to know that he could handle her so he inched up closer and grabbed her ass, halting her from moving. He began punishing her with each gut twisting thrust. Bossee could feel his dick so far inside of her, it almost made her stomach cramp up, but she was loving it.

"Oooohhhhh shitt!" she hollered out, not caring how loud she was.

Rory was fucking her like Kane had never did.

She felt the pressure rise in her love box so, she welcomed yet another orgasm. She was in total bliss, but Rory seemed to just be getting started. He slowed down a little but never stopped stroking, building up another nut for Bossee.

"This is some good ass pussy," Rory hissed as he continued.

He was trying to prove a point to her, but he was now losing the battle with holding back his nut.

"Yeaaaaaahhhhh, this my pussy," Rory uttered as the warm semen shot out inside of her.

Rory felt like the man when he pulled out his dick, slowly, because Bossee couldn't move. She was stuck in that position and had nodded off almost immediately. He eased into the bathroom to get her a warm rag and cleaned her up while her ass was still tooted in the air. He got in bed and pulled her up close to him, she never woke up. Soon Rory drifted off to sleep, a happy man.

CHAPTER SEVENTEEN

The following day, Bossee woke up refreshed. Looking over at Rory a smile crept across her lips, reaching over she kissed his sleeping face until his eyes opened. He now wore a smile.

"Morning boo," Rory mumbled as he sat up and stretched.

They both sat up in the bed quiet for a moment, each with thoughts from last night.

"Today is the day," Bossee blurted out.

Rory knew what she meant but chose to keep his thoughts to himself.

"I'm about gather myself so we can head out boo," Rory let her know, getting up to go to the bathroom.

Bossee sat in the bed for a couple more minutes thinking about Kane and Torrica. *Fuck both of them,* she thought as shook her head. Bossee decided to take a shower in the other bathroom, so she gathered everything that she needed.

An hour and thirty minutes later Rory, Trendini, Nezzy, and Bossee were seated in Bossee's truck, outside of the Bitch Mansion.

"You sure they still at the hotel, Nez," Bossee asked her as they passed the blunt back and forth.

"Girl, yeah with their trifling asses. I forgot to tell you I placed a GPS tracker on both of their cars last night. See," Nezzy said in a matter of fact manner as she tapped the app.

The GPS showed that both cars were still idle at the hotel. Bossee grabbed the phone and smiled, her friend always was steps ahead of an enemy. Bossee handed the phone back to her, then she leaned over to the driver seat and pecked Rory on his lips.

"Come on," Rory said so they all, excluding Trendini, exited the truck.

She was to stay in the truck and be the lookout. They parked in the garage so they could move back and forth without anyone seeing them.

Bossee opened the door that lead to the kitchen and lead them upstairs to Kane's office. They spoke no words, they were all in goon mode and wanted payback, *each for their own reasons.* Bossee removed the giant painting that was hanging on the wall behind his desk.

To the average eye it looked as nothing was there, but it was a tiny button she pressed. Rory and Nezzy was startled as the fireplace made a buzzing noise and flipped open. Bossee walked to the fireplace and lifted the door lever.

"Let's get to it," she said as the steps were now visible.

Rory was kind of impressed with the trap door, it was complexed. Once they reached the bottom Rory got pissed off. He immediately identified his work to the left of the room on a folding table.

He knew that it belonged to him because of the scorpion stamp on the packaging. This work costed his young nephews their lives. The entire room was filled with so many blocks of coke that it looked like something from a movie. Bossee knew exactly how much Kane had already, but Nezzy and Rory was shocked.

"Okay, it's a door that leads to the garage over there. Here," Bossee instructed as she passed them huge empty duffle bags.

They all began stuffing the bags with as much as they could before taking it to the truck. They each made six trips back and forth to the truck with bags of dope and money.

"Damn, Kane had all this coke?" Trendini exclaimed when they walked to the truck for the sixth time.

The truck was loaded to the max, they barely had room to sit in the backseat. Rory wasn't too fond of Trendini because she looked like the girl he shot. So, he sat in the front and stayed on point while side eyeing her. Bossee told him that it was her twin, but in his mind she couldn't be trusted. Bossee had explained to him on the way to get her that she was cool, but he wasn't feeling it.

"Okay Twin, we about to take you to Rory's warehouse then go handle the other situation. He has some workers over there to unload the truck, you watch everything while they do," Nezzy said breaking the silence.

"Bet. Aye Bossee, don't kill her, okay?" Trendini mumbled with her head down.

She knew her sister fucked up royally, so this was the price she had to pay.

"I told you what's up. She is still family, but fuck Kane," Bossee spat.

They pulled up to the warehouse that belonged to Rory, a couple minutes later. They had another car waiting for them, so they all exited the truck after Rory parked and got in the Benz that was waiting with no plates.

"You sure you trust her?" Rory exclaimed with frowns in his forehead as he gazed at Trendini calling shots to his workers. His workers knew she was in charge, but this was the first time Rory he had ever let a female call the shots at his warehouse.

However, most of the work was Bossee's so he trusted her judgement.

"Yes, Rory. Her and Nezzy are cool, and after I deliver this ass whooping to her twin, she will be back cool too. I promise."

Rory nodded and drove off. He heard what she was saying but he was going to have his personal eye on her...

*****

"It's open," Nezzy said as she used her tools to open the hotel's door to Kane and Torrica's room.

Nezzy knew which one because she paid a housekeeper for the information earlier. The trio crept in quietly, and stood in the foyer area. Bossee flipped at the sight of Torrica laying on her stomach, stretched out sleeping peacefully. Bossee scanned the room and didn't see Kane, but the shower turning on alerted them that he was there. An evil smile crept on Rory's face, he wanted Kane so bad his hands trembled.

"Shhhhhh…" Bossee hissed as she placed her index finger to her mouth.
She signaled for Rory to watch the door. She peeped that Kane's pistol was on the nightstand, so she knew they had gotten the drop on him.

"Wake up bitch," Bossee said as she stood over Torrica.

She placed Torrica in a headlock, as she sat on top of her. Torrica tried to flip over but Bossee had all her weight on her.

"Wait…" Torrica tried to say but Bossee was choking her and she couldn't breathe. Bossee kept her left arm around her neck and started chopping her in the back of the head with her right fist. The brass knuckles she wore made each hit sound out loudly.

After she had beaten her head up until she saw blood, Bossee stood up and dragged her out the bed by her hair. As soon as her body hit the floor with a thump, Nezzy started stomping her in the sides.

"Pleaseee stop," Torrica muttered. She couldn't figure out why her voice wasn't coming out.

She wanted to scream but she couldn't. The hits to the back of her had her dizzy, and she was scared. She hadn't yet saw who was attacking her. She was now on her back on the floor, when she saw Bossee's face, she almost pissed herself.

"Bitchhh..." Bossee growled as she sat back on top of her and punched her repeatedly in the face and head.

Bossee had blacked out, she missed and hit Nezzy's arm. Nezzy was holding Torrica down by the neck, trying her best to squeeze the life out of her.

"Damn bitch, you chopped my damn arm," Nezzy said jerking her arm back. Nezzy let her guard down a little so Torrica was able to hit Nezzy. Torrica's hit was hard as fuck, and it pissed her off. She hopped up and started kicking Torrica where she could. Nezzy wanted more action so she took the police baton she brought along and started chopping Torrica on the ankles and legs.

"This bitch ass nigga in here shooting up dope," Rory yelled. He was anxious to get Kane, so he snuck to the bathroom while Bossee and Nezzy whipped Torrica's ass.

Kane was sitting on the toilet in a nod, with the needle still in his arm. Rory walked over casually. With all he had in him, he punched Kane. Kane's already limp body flew into the running shower. Kane's eyes popped open from the blow, now he was looking directly into his enemies eyes. Rory hopped over his body not caring about getting wet.

"I finally found your bitch ass, and it took for you to fuck your wife's cousin for me to find your dumbass," Rory gritted in his face.

"What you say, nigga? You fuckin' my bitch?" Kane asked slightly dazed, but still keeping his *I don't give a fuck* attitude.

Rory took his 9mm and pistol whipped him across the face.

"I'm doing more than fuckin' your bitch, nigga."

"She'll never bow down to you, nigga. She'll never forget me no matter how much dick you put in her. She just going to kill you off for the next dope nigga. She ain't shit!" he spat blood in Rory's face that sent his temper through the roof.

Pop pop pop

The blows Rory delivered to Kane landed on and around his temple. Kane was knocked out by the first blow, but Rory continued to hit him in the same area. He wanted to beat him to death, so he hit him countless times until he saw him take his last breath. He then reached over and snatched every chain off Kane's neck and stuffed them in his pocket. He stepped out the shower, soaked in water. He sat on the toilet to catch his breath. Rory was so worked up that he didn't notice when Bossee came in the bathroom. She was in there while Rory was beating him.

"Come on babe, it's time to go," Bossee said as she eyed Kane's body in total shock.

She had never seen him so helpless and it sort of made her feel weak. She felt like her life was powered by Kane at one point, now he was gone because of lies and greed. She saw him as the strongest man she knew, now she saw him at his weakest. *Damn,* she said under her breath. She took the gun from Rory and led him out to the bedroom with a drying towel.

"Let's go…" she uttered before she snapped back into beast mode.

Nezzy had Torrica hogtied, she was now passed out. Bossee took the work she brought with them out of her bag and sprinkled on the floor in different areas. Her, Nezzy, and Rory pulled Kane's body from the tub, dragging it to the front. Nezzy took a few one hundred-dollar bills and put them near Kane's pocket. She made sure to turn one of his pockets inside out. The trio went around the room, turning random things over near Kane's body making the scene look like a robbery. They wore gloves so they didn't have to worry about what they touched.

"Bring this bitch to the car," Bossee said about Torrica as she opened the door to leave.

Thankfully, the hotel wasn't indoors so Rory helped Nezzy carry Torrica to the car with a blanket over her. Nezzy laid her in the back seat and got in. Bossee got in the passenger and Rory drove off.

"Take me back to where we got the work from," Bossee said as she took her phone out her pocket and dialed a number.

"What's up, Allaysia?" You need me now?" her cousin, Wanda, said when she picked up her phone.

Bossee had her oldest cousin on standby to nurse Torrica back to health without anybody in their business. Wanda was a PA at Martin Luther King Hospital in Compton. She did house calls like this on the side. She was always on call with her medicine bag for all the top dope boys that got shot and didn't want to be seen in a hospital. So, Allaysia knew exactly who to call. As bad as she wanted to kill Torrica's ass, she knew she couldn't. They were blood, and she loved Trendini and her aunt to the core, so she just decided to teach Torrica a big lesson about crossing the ones that love her.

"Yeah, I'm on my way to the address I gave you last night. So, come A.S.A.P. She's in bad shape," Bossee said as she shook her head and rubbed her aching knuckles.

"Well that serves her right. Torrica always has to be the one to do dumb shit, out of all of us," Wanda expressed.

Her and Bossee's family was big and full of girls. They all had their flaws but Torrica had the disloyalty flaw that nobody in the family liked or knew about.

"You know I know, cousin. I'll see you soon."

Bossee dismissed her call. The ride to the mansion was silent as everyone got lost in their own worlds. Twenty minutes later Rory was pulling up the driveway of the house. He killed the engine.

"I'm probably going to be in here for a while. You want to come in or meet me later?" Bossee asked as she gazed at Rory.

Nezzy had stepped out to smoke a Newport. Rory looked at the house and shook his head. Knowing it was Kane's spot, he wanted nothing to do with anything in the house at that point.

"Nah, I gotta go get with my fam and tell em the news. Thank you tho, babe. You did your thing in there," he reached over and kissed her.

"You're welcome, that nigga got what he deserved, and my cousin. Thank you for handling that nigga. Now I can move on once this nigga is in the ground," she opened the car door, "I'll be at your spot later. I have to get my daughter though, she's been texting me."

"Alright cool, more than likely I'm going to have my daughter too. She's my peace," Rory responded.

They kissed once more, and then Nezzy and Bossee took Torrica inside. Rory took off to his hood. He felt good knowing Kane was dead by his hands. He knew his nephews could rest in peace now...

*****

A day later...

After Trendini got the news that Bossee didn't kill her twin, she could breathe again. However, the damage that was done would scar her for a lifetime. The pictures Nezzy sent her had tears falling from her eyes. Trendini didn't let too much make her cry, but seeing her twin out cold, had her a bit in a panic.

Nezzy: She's at the mansion with a nurse.

Nezzy texted back after she sent the pictures. Thanking God, she wasn't just laid in a hospital suffering, she quickly dressed and hopped in her brand-new white Lamborghini.

She raced through the streets of Los Angeles on the sleek wet road in deep thought. She was hoping her twin learned her lesson and knew not to do any fuck shit anymore to family.

Trendini pulled into one of the mansions many parking spaces inside the garage. She took a deep breath before getting out and going inside. When she entered, she saw Bossee talking on the phone cooking. Bossee acknowledged her presence by pointing to the room at the end of the hall on the first floor.

Trendini shook her head to gesture that she understood what she was saying, so she made her way back. Trendini walked in and gasped at the sight of her sister. Her face was double its normal size and her eyes were swollen. She was so black and blue that Trendini knew that it would be months before she healed.

"Who's there?" Torrica asked, hearing the door open.

She had woken up two hours ago, and had yet to hear anyone come in. Her windpipe was damaged, she discovered she couldn't yell for help, so she just laid there crying. She couldn't lift her legs either because Nezzy broke one with the baton.

"It's me sis," Trendini whimpered with her own fresh tears falling.

"Oh my God, someone kidnapped me sis. I'm so glad you found me," Torrica hoarsely voiced.

She was still confused about what had happened, she thought she remembered seeing Bossee but she wasn't sure if she was tripping.

"Nah sis, you fucked up. Bossee found out you fucked Kane. Twin, why you keep doing all this fucked up shit? Bossee changed our lifestyle. We were fucking all kinds of niggas for money before she came back and put us on. Now look at you. Her and Nezzy whooped your ass. I had to beg her not to kill you," Trendini schooled her with anger.

Tears sprang from Torrica's puffy eyes as her sister spoke. She was grateful that Bossee didn't kill her because she knew how evil her cousin could get.

"Where's Kane?" Torrica asked.

"Dead..." Bossee answered the question for Torrica as she stepped in.

Bossee couldn't believe that was the first thing she had to say after being out over twenty-four hours. Kane really had Torrica's mind gone.

"Good, because I was going to kill him anyway to prove a point. I fucked up cousin, I'm sorry," Torrica cried.

She meant what she said but she was also sad that Kane was dead. She had really fallen for him, but she knew she was in the wrong. The ass whooping her body endured was enough to get her to see how fucked up her ways was.

"I spared your life this time, because you are family regardless. I only beat your ass, but on God I wanted to squeeze the life out of you. You will be okay though, I have someone taking care of you around the clock. That's what family does. You need to learn what loyalty is, Torrica. Loyalty is an action, you can love or hate someone and still have their back," Bossee said without any regrets.

Bossee left the room to let the twins have their moment. She prayed her words sunk in her cousin's head before she ended up dead somewhere.

"You knew about them plotting on me?" Torrica asked trying to put all the pieces together in her head.

"Yeah, I told you I begged for your life. But fuck all that, you're going to live. Hopefully you learned a lesson, but I have a gift for you. While you were running around, I made a move to put us in position. You remember we had always talked about T&T? Well, it's up and ready for a grand opening," Trendini said.

"Our clothing store?" Torrica asked making sure she had heard her right.

They had said since they were little girls that they would open a designer boutique. Torrica let everything sink in and the room grew silent for a few minutes.

"Thank you, sis. Let's live out our dreams," Torrica finally said.

She was happy her sister had been smarter than her with the money they had made. Torrica hadn't saved a penny of hers. She figured Kane would've taken care of her like he told her. Torrica silently said a prayer for Kane's and their baby's soul, she also said a thank you for her sister.

CHAPTER EIGHTEEN

Two weeks later.

Kane's funeral.

Life had been crazy yet peaceful since Kane's death. All his family members were scrambling trying to find out who killed him, but they came up short because they had no idea what was going on in California. Bossee was fully settled with Rory, but since she was still married to Kane, she had to take care of funeral arrangements with his family. She didn't want to look suspicious, however she knew she wouldn't because Kane's family loved her and knew that she was his ride or die. Therefore, she was now on a private flight back to South Carolina with Kane's body in a compartment under the plane. She figured she would bury him in his hometown and be done with it.

Her private jet landed in South Carolina on a Friday at five in the evening. Bossee stepped off the plane wearing a black Chanel pant suit with matching black suede stilettos and huge dark Chanel shades. She stepped down the steps of the plane with her carry on and walked over to her awaiting Mercedes car service.

"So, are we taking the body to the funeral home so they can start getting him ready?" one of Rory's goons said as he walked behind her.

Rory wasn't taking any chances with Bossee going to S.C. alone, so he sent one of his men.

"Yes..." she responded nonchalantly as she opened the door to the car.

She then saw a van pull on the runway as well. She knew it was the transportation to pick up Kane.

"It's almost over," she mumbled to herself as they took Kane's body from the plane.

He was in a silver casket like he wanted with 14k gold trimming. She shook her head as she watched them put him in the back of the van. He wasn't to be in a hearse until the funeral the following morning.

After they put him in the van, she told her driver to drive off.

She had business to handle, so she told the driver to take her downtown to Kane's lawyer's office. Kane had a will and a fat insurance policy that was in her name and she was ready to take the steps to cash out. Bossee's driver pulled up in front of Kane's lawyer's office twenty minutes later. Bossee looked out the window and saw Kane's mother standing in front of the office. She sighed, although she knew she was coming.

She was wearing a black church dress and black kitten heels. Bossee knew his mother was hurt, that was her baby boy. But she had no idea the demons her son carried.

"I'll be out in an hour, so don't leave," she told the driver.

He nodded. Bossee stepped out and walked over to Kane's mother, Ms. Smith. Bossee told her to meet her so that they could go over everything regarding

Kane's assets. Bossee figured she would give his mother some stuff because she was good peoples.

"Oh, Allaysia, I've been dying to see you. Who would do this to Derell?" she cried out as Bossee took her in her arms.

"I don't know, Ms. Smith, he's in a better place now though," Bossee expressed.

"I know, but he was so young, and Keyley is going to be devastated without her father. Is she here?" Ms. Smith asked as she gazed at Bossee.

"She'll be here tomorrow with my mother… Let's go inside though, it's getting late."

Bossee really didn't want to drag her daughter into all of the drama that was going on, but this was the only way she could see herself telling her and moving on. For a long time, she noticed her daughter never had a real connection with her father so she knew it would probably be easy to break the news to her. She was only four, so she felt like she had time to grow out of the experience of seeing her father in a casket. Bossee was thankful her daughter loved her to the core because she knew she could be better and was going to do better.

The two walked into the single office. The layer's receptionist walked them to the back. When they walked in, Kane's lawyer, Toler, was sitting at his desk pulling files from a manila folder. Bossee and Ms. Smith sat at his desk and he got straight to it.

"Ms. Smith, this is his will, I know you are familiar with it so I will let you look over it." He slid her a notarized paper that she remembered signing five years ago. A year after they got together Kane made his will because he knew he was too heavy in the streets to not have one. He signed everything over to Bossee.

Every time he got something of value, he added it to the list. Bossee was to get whatever she wanted and give the rest to his mother.

"Mama Smith, you can have all his cars that he left here and the estate we had here. I'll take everything in California and give you two of the eight million I have on the policy," Bossee said as she continued to look at the paper.

Bossee didn't want any bad karma on her, so she gave his mother what she already knew she wanted. She had loved their house in South Carolina since they had gotten it and now it was hers to move into.

"Okay, thank you," she smiled and nodded.

An hour later, Bossee was in her hotel room, sitting in silence yet again. She'd been having so many sleepless nights, and she knew this one would be another. She decided to light a few candles and take a hot shower. Bossee let the warm water hit her face as her tears ran freely. Every time she was alone, she thought about Kane. He was her husband and the scar he left on her heart, she knew it would always be there.

"How could you do this to me, Kane?" she cried out in a low whimper.

She looked down at her stomach and rubbed her flat belly. She had taken a pregnancy test before her flight and found out that she was pregnant.

She knew she was a few weeks pregnant by Kane and there was no way she was keeping it. Keyley was the only reminder she wanted of Kane. She knew it was his because Kane busts nuts in her all the time. She was moving on and starting fresh. She wasn't telling anyone about her appointment she had first thing Monday morning. It was something she was taking to her grave. Bossee sucked up her tears and washed with her lavender soap. She stepped out and dried off.

Skipping clothes, she drowned the rest of her tears in a bottle of wine. Before she knew it, she was sitting front row at Kane's casket in his hometown church. Bossee was wearing a long black dress and her black Chanel shades. She dressed her daughter in a puffy black dress and black patent leather shoes. His whole family was there, crying and praying. She looked over at her daughter and she showed no emotion. She reached over and whispered in her ear.

"Are you okay?" she asked her daughter.

"Yes, I want to go play outside in the grass, I'm bored," she whispered back.

"We're leaving in a minute, okay. You have to say goodbye to your father."

Keyley crossed her arms, she had no interest in what was going on. She didn't cry or show any emotion when Bossee walked her to the casket. That was more validation for Bossee to move on.

"Your own damn daughter knows you're grimy, Kane," she whispered in his casket and walked off.

*****

Burn party... Two days later

Bossee felt good being back in California. She felt like a free woman with her name back, now it was time to collect all the shit she inherited from Kane and dispose of it. Kane had left her everything down to his draws, and she had no use for any of his things. Kane had so much expensive shit, but it didn't move her one bit. She decided to sell all his cars, his estates, and his jewelry, but she still had his clothes.

She knew Rory wouldn't accept anything that belonged to Kane and she didn't want anyone wearing his demons, so she decided not to donate it. She decided to have a *Burn Party* and use it as a celebration. Bossee took an Uber to U-Haul and rented a midsize truck. She took it home and emptied out his walk-in closet. All his shoes, clothes, jackets, belts, draws, everything... *she loaded it up*.

Bossee was dog tired after lugging all his clothes through the house. She flopped on her porch and pulled her phone from her bra. She sent Nezzy a text.

Meet me in the desert at midnight. We're having a Burn Party…

Nezzy Boo: A Burn Party? What the fuck is that, bitch?! LOL

I'm taking all Kane's shit to the desert and burning all his demons. Bring a bottle of Jack Daniels and D'usse. We gettin fucked up!

Nezzy Boo: OMG Bossee, I swear you ain't shit but I love it. What's the location, bitch?
The desert, bitch. Where Flex is buried…

Nezzy Boo: Fasho, I'm there.

Midnight was approaching fast after Bossee lounged around the house in silence. She dressed in a black mini dress that looked like it was painted on her, and a pair of Louboutin Kate Pete edition ankle boot stilettos. She made sure she didn't wear any panties just for the hell of it and bright red lipstick. Kane hated when she didn't wear panties or wore red lipstick, now she was doing the things she liked to do.

"Ain't no nigga stopping me from doing what I want to do this go round, I'm Bossee," she exclaimed as she gazed at herself in the mirror and applied her lipstick extra thick.

Bossee walked outside and hopped in the U-Haul. She looked like she needed to be behind the wheel of her new Ferrari. As she drove, she texted Torrica. Over the last two weeks while she was healing, her and Bossee had been talking, a lot.

Torrica told Bossee how Kane had gotten out of control and planned on not paying the girls, or Bossee, anymore. He had fallen heavy to Meth, and pills, and Torrica was caught in his trap. He went from not wanting her, to not wanting her to leave him, and Torrica knew it was the drugs. She was serious about planning to kill him but she didn't know how she was going to do it.

Bossee knew Kane had a drug problem, she knew he played with his nose from time to time and popped Xanax, but she didn't think it was that bad to the point where he was shooting up Meth. That was why she hardly let him around their daughter because she never knew when he was heavy in his addiction. He kept it from Bossee, but she always caught him and knew when he was high off more than weed. So much was wrong about her marriage and she allowed a lot of it to happen, but she vowed nothing like Kane would ever be let in her life again.

Come out side and bring ya crutches. Get a lil cute too, we going to a party.

Torrica: A party? Okay, give me fifteen minutes.

Fifteen minutes later, Torrica came out the trap mansion dressed for the occasion. She had on a one-piece white spandex bodysuit and a white fur jacket that stopped at her waist. The swelling was down in her face, so she was able to wear makeup over her scars. She had her blonde lace wig bob with bangs covering her eyes, so people wouldn't notice the red spots in her eyes from the blood vessels that were busted. She was wearing one Air Max on one foot and her other was in a cast still.

Torrica limped over to the truck while shaking her head. Bossee flew the door open with a huge smile on her face.

"No way," Torrica said when she looked at the truck and then at Bossee.

"Where the fuck we going in this, Bossee?" Torrica turned up her nose.

She didn't want to be caught dead in a U-Haul going to a party.

"What? You can't take a ride with ya *favorite cousin* in a U-Haul to a party? You that boujee now?"

"You're, crazy Bossee. But let's go."

The ride was full of weed smoke and loud music on their way to Barstow. Her and Torrica were smoking so much weed, she didn't notice they were driving way out. Torrica turned the music down.

"Allaysia, where the fuck is this party? We almost to Vegas in this damn U-Haul," Torrica expressed as she continued to look around.

Bossee smirked, "You'll see."

A weary feeling came over Torrica, but she didn't say a word. An hour later, Bossee was driving through a dark desert area in the middle of nowhere. *You've arrived at your destination,* her GPS said on her phone. That's when Torrica really got scared. *This bitch is finna kill me...*

"Look, Bossee, if you are bringing me out here to kill me, let's get it over with, even though I was serious when I said I learned my lesson," Torrica said in a shaky tone.

Bossee laughed, "nah, I brought you here for therapy, get out."

Torrica sighed. She didn't know what Bossee was talking about, but she was glad it wasn't about her death.

"It was easy getting in, but I need help getting out."

Bossee got out and helped Torrica. No sooner than they walked to the back of the truck, she saw the bright head lights on Nezzy's Ferrari. Her and

Bossee had bought matching cars. As she got closer, they heard her loud music playing. Nezzy drove up full speed on the side of the truck and hopped out with her bottle of D'usse open.

"What up, Bossee? You ready to get this burn party cracking? Oh shit, what is she doing here? We finna burn her ass too?" Nezzy joked as she took a swig of the liquor.

She was already loaded because she was drinking her whole two-hour drive.

"Burn Party? and hell nah, she already said I ain't here to die," Torrica expressed in a serious tone.

"I'm just playing, bitch! Lighten up! So, what's up B, you ready?" Nezzy asked.

"Yup," She pulled up the back of the truck.

When Torrica laid eyes on all the men's clothing, she immediately knew who they belonged to. She saw shoes and clothes she had seen him in, and she could even smell his cologne reeking from the truck. Memories of her and Kane flooded her brain at that very moment. She took in the sight and smell of his clothes and sighed to herself. *This nigga just won't shake me,* she thought.

"I'm sure you know who clothes these are," Bossee said as she gazed at Torrica gazing inside of the truck.

"Yes, I know," Torrica answered, trying to sound like she was unbothered, but truthfully as much as she hated him for the damage he caused, he still had a slight tug on her heart.

"Nezzy, help me pull all this shit out and make a pyramid. Torrica, we're about to set it on fire and let it burn, we letting Kane go for good…"

Torrica nodded. Minutes later, Bossee was handing Nezzy and Torrica a can of lighter fluid and matches. The girls walked around the pyramid of clothes and poured the fluid all over it. Bossee lit the first match and the girls followed behind her. Within seconds the clothes went up into flames.

"Pop another bottle, Nezzy, Torrica roll a blunt. We're having a bonfire with this nigga shit," Bossee expressed as she looked at the flames.

"Okay!" Torrica said slightly more excited than she was when she first arrived.

Bossee was right, she needed to let Kane burn. He never loved her, he used her for what he could get out of her and that was pussy and her talent she had in the streets. She needed him off her heart and off her mental, so she danced around the fire with Nezzy and Bossee as trap music played loudly from Nezzy's Ferrari.

"Hold up, this my shit!" Nezzy said as she rushed over to her car and turned up the music louder.

Ball w/o You by 21 Savage came blaring through her crystal, clear speakers.

I gave you my all.

You was my dawg.

I would have went to war with the world on your call (On your call)

Thought you had my back (Nah)

You let me fall (Let me fall)

You healed my pain (My pain)

Then you caused it (Then you caused it)

Now I gotta ball without you (Straight up)

Bossee and Nezzy rapped the lyrics to the song as her and Bossee poured liquor into the fire, making it flame out of control. They laughed and stepped back making sure they didn't get burned. Bossee glanced over at Torrica. She was looking out at the many stars in her own world. Bossee walked over to her and hugged her. Soon as Torrica felt her cousin's touch she fell into her embrace. She cried without saying a word.

"You gotta let it go, T, it's over now," Bossee said to her cousin.

One thing that Bossee knew about Kane was that he had a weird hold on women. She never understood it. Every woman he had cheated on her with were left with some kind of love for him. An hour later the fire was going out, so the girls headed back. When Bossee pulled in front of the mansion, the sun was coming up. Torrica was drunk and so was Bossee.

"Thank you for inviting me out, Bossee. I needed that," Torrica said as she gazed at Bossee.

"You're welcome, I hope now you know not to mess with anybody else's man. It was only easy for you because I know what kind of nigga Kane was and how he had an effect on bitches. But next time if you ever try some shit like you did, I will kill you bitch. I forgive you and I love you, but that trust shit is broken."

Torrica sighed. She hated the position she was in with her cousin, but she knew it was all her fault.

"I hear you, and I'm sorry again."

"Oh yeah, this house is going up for sale. You have to go back to your condo with Trendini within a month."

"Okay, I'm ready to go home anyway. The house is creepy now."

Bossee helped Torrica out and went on home. She felt good. She had all of Kane's clothing away from her, now she had to make arrangements to sell his estates and jewelry. She was using the money to get a new house...

EPILOGUE

One year later

"What color do you want your toes, Keyley? Same color as Royal or different?" Bossee asked her daughter.

They were sitting outside in her backyard and she was painting their toes. It was a nice summer afternoon, so she took her daughter and Rory's daughter to their backyard for some sun. Bossee was finally feeling at peace and she was able to sleep again. After Kane's death, she fell into a depression that she tried to ignore, but Rory spotted it immediately when he saw her sitting up crying for nights at a time. He understood and let her grieve but he also put her through counselling.

Now a year later, she had come to the realization that her life was different but in a good way. She was now a better mother and was starting to take interest in just being a stay at home mom. She even thought about going back to school. Rory and Nezzy were now running things so she had more time to be at home with the kids and continue her education. She was so grateful Rory didn't leave her in her time of grief and helped her become a better woman.

"No, I want red like you, mommy," Keyley replied with a smile.

"No, baby you get pink or purple. No red."

"Okay, pink," she said handing her mom a pink glitter polish.

As Bossee painted Keyley's toes, Rory walked outside to see his favorite girls. Rory loved coming home to his new house every day to his new little family. He made sure he came home every day and made sure they were okay. His daughter had been staying with Bossee while she stayed home with Keyley because Rory was going through a custody battle. Rory got to know Bossee's daughter and she got to know his, so they were one little happy family.

"Y'all out here having a party without me," Rory smiled as he picked up a few crackers from the tray Bossee had brought outside with cheese, meat, crackers, and grapes.

"We didn't know you were coming home this early. You want your toes polished?" Bossee joked.

The girls laughed.

"Yeah, dad, let me polish your toes," Royal said.

She was seven years old.

"Nah, you know I don't get down like that. But can you come inside for a minute, Allaysia, I want to talk to you."

"Okay, girls, let your toes dry and then put on your sandals. When I finish talking to daddy, y'all are going with me to T&T," Bossee stood up.

"Yes! We love T&T!" the girls boasted.

They loved the twins store because they had a kid's section and they let them get whatever they wanted. Bossee and Rory walked into the house and stood in the kitchen.

"So, you gonna finally tell ya homegirls about this baby shower you've been putting together for our young king?" Rory asked as he rubbed her belly.

Bossee was five months pregnant with his first son and she was feeling good about it. After aborting Kane's baby, she wasn't sure if she wanted another. Rory knew nothing about her abortion or how she felt about having another. But he had proven to her he would be a good dad and be nothing like Kane. Plus, she knew with all the love making she was receiving from Rory, it was bound to happen and there was no way she was aborting his baby.

However, she had been keeping her pregnancy from The Bitch Gang because she didn't want them to baby her, but now she was ready to tell them because she was planning a huge baby shower.

"Yes, I'm going to break the news to them that I'm pregnant."

Rory laughed, "you look like you are carrying a soccer ball in your stomach and you been walking around in sweaters in the summer like a pregnant teenager. You really think they don't know?" he raised his eyebrow.

"Ain't nobody said nothing, they don't know."

Rory shook his head and laughed.

"Well I got some great fucking news that's why I'm home early. I got full custody of Royal today. Her mother didn't complete any of the classes like she was supposed to and failed her drug test."

Bossee brought her hand to her mouth in shock. She knew how bad Rory wanted custody of his daughter. She had heard the constant arguments and been to a couple court hearings, so she knew his story well.

"I'm so happy for you, it's unfortunate what's going on with her mother. Hopefully she gets it right," she hugged him.

"Well if she doesn't, my daughter has nothing to worry about because she has us."

"I like it when you say us, baby," she smiled and gazed in his eyes.

"If you love hearing it so much, why don't you let me wife you?"

"I will babe. Soon…"

The conversation was cut when the girls ran into the house, which Bossee was glad. She always felt uncomfortable when Rory brought up marriage. She loved him but she wasn't ready for that kind of union again. Her and Rory were in a good space and she didn't want walking down the aisle to mess it up.

"Are we going to T&T now?" the girls asked in unison.

"Yeah let me go get ready."

"Nezzy has your cut from that pick up you set up this morning. I'll see y'all later," he walked off to his home office.

He figured since he would have a couple hours to himself, he was going to make a few phone calls and think of his next move.

After Bossee changed into a cute summer dress, finally showing off her baby bump, her and the girls went to Rory's office and kissed him goodbye. Bossee and the girls got in her Bentley truck and headed to the twins store in Hollywood. She knew all the girls were probably there already because that was their new headquarters. Bossee turned on the latest Kidz Bop album and the girls sang her ears off while she drove on the highway like she was their driver. She loved the bond Keyley and Royal had built over the months. They had been around each other for the last year, and Keyley had been happy ever since to call Royal big sister.

She was only five years old and an only child, so having someone around kept her content and smiling. Twenty minutes later, Bossee was pulling in front of the store. She looked out her passenger window and saw Nezzy, the twins, and one of the twins' associates standing in a circle smoking a blunt. Bossee and the girls got out and walked over to their circle.

"What's up, Bossee? You finally got your ass out the house huh? It must be payday," Trendini teased as Bossee walked the circle and hugged the girls.

"Man, I been sick, but I feel good now, and yes I came to get my cut. I'm glad all y'all here together tho. I want to talk to y'all about something."

The girls walked inside and stood around the cash register area while Royal and Keyley rushed off to the kids' section. The girls looked at Bossee and patiently waited for her to talk.

"So as y'all know, me and Rory have gotten close. He's the reason the Bitch Gang went from enemies of the state to top hustlers in the game, and we want to keep running this shit like a family business."

The girls nodded. She was right. They went from jack girls to being, the plug. Rory had them making connects with dealers from California to New York, and he even plugged them with some people he knew in South Carolina. Bossee had her homegirl Lexy in charge of S.C.

Business was booming better than ever with less violence and more money like Bossee wanted.

"You know we appreciate you Bossee, but what's up?" Nezzy asked as she eyed Bossee.

"Well, me and Rory have decided to add to our family. I'm pregnant, five months to be exact with a baby boy."

The girls looked at each other and started laughing. Bossee had a confused look on her face until Torrica spoke up.

"Girl, what? We already knew you were pregnant. You been in tennis shoes and sweaters all summer and we all know tennis shoes are not your style. We already discussed it."

"Damn, y'all get on my nerves," Bossee rolled her eyes because she knew she had proven Rory right.

"Well I'm having my baby shower next month. It's going to be big, so I'll be sending y'all invitations in the mail. I have everything taken care of, I just need y'all to show up, okay?"

Nezzy beamed with excitement as she rubbed Bossee's belly.

"Oh my god, I can't wait to meet the new baby. I'm so happy for you and Rory, do he have a brother by the way?" Nezzy laughed, but she was serious.

"Actually, he does have an older brother and he's cute. I'm surprised you haven't seen him. He's a part of his operation."

"Shit, well I will be looking for his ass because Rory is a winner," Nezzy teased.

After hearing Bossee come out about her pregnancy, the girls opened a bottle of champagne to celebrate while music played throughout the store. Things had turned around for the good for the Bitch Gang and they were ready to see what the future had in store for them…

TO BE CONTINUED...

Bitch Gang 2 is late summer '19! Tell us who your favorite character was in your customer review!

Dropping in April. Here's a sneak peek!

ROBIN & KASHA

A GANGSTA GIRL AND HER BULLY

CHAPTER ONE

Darrius

"And, I told Keisha she had to bring the champagne. Did you know she declined, talking about we're the ones with all the money; we should buy all the liquor. It's her damn party."

I was sitting in an expensive ass restaurant with my wife listening to her go on and on about how my sister didn't want to pay for champagne for her formal birthday gathering. However, I couldn't even focus on a word she was saying. I had just gotten a text before we stepped inside, telling me that one of my trap houses was robbed. I had to get out of here, but I knew my wife wasn't going for it.

"Well, you know how Keisha is, you know she doesn't have five-grand to splurge on liquor even for her own party. She has five kids and doesn't live the life you live." I said as I sipped my cognac.

"I'm just tired of them always thinking we're supposed to do everything with these gatherings. This was all your mother's idea, now none of them have the money." She crossed her arms.

My wife was so cute when she was mad, but I knew she was serious. I always admired the little things she stressed about, because she had no idea that my problems were way bigger than hers.

"Well, Rocsi, stop showing them so much and start telling them no. I been told you that. MY mom has money, but whatever they don't want to do, I'll handle."

She sighed and picked up her glass of wine. "You're right. Well, I don't want to bore you with the drama and I know you've been working all day. I'm just glad we were able to have a few hours out together."

"Me too…"

Me and my wife sat and ate a delicious meal in silence as the soft music in the restaurant played. My phone was buzzing off the hook in my pocket and I couldn't answer it because it was my second phone, my trap phone. I was a good father and businessman, and I loved my wife to the core… but I lived a life she knew nothing about. My wife thought I was a clean white-collar dude that worked at my office in Manhattan doing stocks and bonds. I did do that, but 60% of my day was dedicated to drug money. My name is D-Boy in the streets. I had a trap house in every borough, and I had to visit them all and meet with my workers every day. But sometimes, I got tied up in my home life like right now.

"Darrius…"

"Yeah, yeah?" I zoned out for a minute thinking about how I was going to get back from the lost I had just taken in the streets. When I looked up Rocsi was putting on her jacket. With my hand on her lower back I led the way out of the restaurant.

I entertained small talk on the drive home although my mind was still elsewhere. When I pulled into our driveway, I cut the engine. It was late so I knew that our two children should have been tucked into their beds sleep. Rosci hopped out of the car and then strutted up our cobblestone driveway towards our home.

Briefly I admired the house that we had built from the ground up. It was hard getting land to work with in Queens, New York but we made it happen. I sighed as I followed behind Rocsi towards the house. In a minute I was going to be back out the door.

“Here, thank you again for the short notice,” Rocsi said to the sitter as she handed the young teenager a hundred-dollar bill.

“Thank you, they are both sound asleep. Same time next Friday?” she asked.

“I’ll let you know okay?” Rocsi said as she closed the door behind the babysitter.

Knowing that I needed to lay my eyes on my angels before I stepped out for the night I headed up our spiral stairs. Rocsi followed closely behind me. I was hoping she didn’t want me to shower and go to bed with her because I had business that needed my attention. Me and Rocsi walked into our kids' room to see that they were sound asleep with their unicorn night light on. They were at the that stage where the darkness was filled with monsters, so we always made sure to keep a little light on for them. We had twin girls and they were my world.

"They look like angels when they are sleep, but are such terrors when they are up," my wife stated with her arms crossed while smiling. I laughed a little because it was true.

"They my babies tho, they can have the world," I whispered not to wake them.

"Well, I'm going to study a little for my exam tomorrow and then I'm going to bed. What are you about to do?" my wife asked as we walked out the kids' room.

"I'm about to head out. My boy Solo invited me to the bar for a drink."

We walked into our room.

"Okay, well I guess I'll see you sometime tomorrow. I'll be sleep when you come home, and I'm know we won't see each other in the morning."

"Alright, but tomorrow night I want you in bed naked when I come home from work." I walked up to my wife and grabbed her by the waist. Her 5'4 frame was stacked in her tight mini dress. Even in her six-inch stilettos, she was still a shorty to me because I was 6'3.

"I thought that was happening tonight, but I guess I can wait." She got on her tippy toes and kissed me. Her peck turned into lots of tongue action, causing my manhood to rise. I backed away because I knew it was never a quickie with my wife.

"It's definitely happening tomorrow night. I'm ready to make our next set of twins with your fine ass."

"Boy, you know we don't need no more kids right now," she said as she smirked.

We disconnected from our embrace and then walked into our huge walk in closet to change. I slipped on something more casual. Balmain jeans, long sleeve

Ralph Lauren shirt, and some Giuseppe Zanotti's was my attire. I kissed my wife goodbye and then sprinted out the house. As soon as I got in the car, my phone started vibrating on my driver side floor. I had forgotten that it had fallen out of my pocket when I got in.

I looked at my call log, I had 50 missed calls and 30 texts from everybody on my team.

I decided to call my lady friend, Ava, that worked with me in this business. She controlled all my spots, and from what I was reading, she was there when my spot in Brownsville had got robbed. Majority of the calls were from her, and the base in her tone when I finally answered the phone let me know that she was on fire.

"Nigga, where the FUCK YOU BEEN? The spot got robbed and you ignoring calls!" she shouted through the phone.

"First of all… curve your fucking tongue while talking to me!" I barked while I turned out of my driveway, "I'm on my way to you now."

I hung up on her and then turned my stereo up. I knew that once I made it to Ava that she would chew me up. Along with running my business while I wasn't present she oversaw my money too. Rocsi was my wife but Ava… she was my *down ass bitch.*

Coming soon From Kasha Diaz

YAYO

Knocking on the door to the guest room that Kasha was staying in, I was a bit nervous.

"Open it!" I heard her sexy ass say.

Walking in, I had to adjust my dick because shawty is raw as fuck in her outfit. Baby girl had on an all-white patent leather tube top and skirt that hugged every curve, along with white Louboutin stilettoes. I forgot what the fuck I came in this room for, but shit, now I wanted to fuck.

"I'm almost ready for the meeting with your crew, did you need something?" I heard her say.

"Damn, baby girl you bad as fuck," I let her know while staring in her eyes.

Walking over to me, she grabbed my dick with a smirk.

"Is that right, Yayo?" she hissed.

That had me smirking to my damn self because this thick ass log caught her by surprise. I could tell because she jerked her hand back fast.

"Fuck yeah," I let roll off my tongue.

"Well, thank you sir," she said just above a whisper, all shy like.

I guess this dick had her scared. I knew her type though. She was used to bossing up on niggas. But when, *YES WHEN*, I put this dick in her life, I'll show her who's boss around this motherfucker. I always get what the fuck I want, and I want Ms. Kasha something terrible. She had her hair pulled up in a bun, so I went to stroke her face, again an electric shock went through my body.

Why the fuck this keep happening? Is this a sign? If so, I'm going to find out. This is the second time it happened since she'd been here. The thing that really intrigued me was her eye contact, it was as though she looked through you. It didn't help that her eyes were a beautiful shade of light hazel. I found myself getting nervous when she gazed at me, and I'm not the type of man to be intimidated.

I've killed more people than I care to admit. So, I'm definitely not scared of her. It's just something about shawty though, I can't explain it. Just know shit was about to get real, because I'm going to shoot my shot.

"Come on, future wife," I said on the slick. Taking another look at shawty had me wanting to fuck her right here. In due time, I was going to train her ass to be my queen.

"Nigga, bring your ass on, we have money to make," she said, turning me on even more.

Watching her twist her sexy ass down the stairs and to the door, I fell in love. Not literally, because I'm a thug, but shit I wanted her ass.

I set the meeting up at a strip joint that my partna owns called, *The Office*. I had all the coke Auntie and the family needs, but they will be needing a route. So, I was going to introduce wifey to my nigga LT and get that situated. After helping her get into my custom chrome Bugatti Chiron, I smashed to the club. We made small talk on the way there, but I could tell that she was in her boss lady zone. Pulling up, I saw all the bucket bitches eyeing my whip. Pulling up to the front, I let my nigga Tone park.

"Come on sweetheart," I said, guiding her by her small waist.

Inside was a zoovie for real, it was a lot of fake ass everywhere. Paying attention to Kasha, I noticed she seemed content and comfortable. Occasionally, I saw her adjust her skirt over her bullet wound, but other than that she was coolin'.

"We can get straight to business now, or we can chill for a few," I said in her ear so she could hear me above the music.

"Nah, let's get to business, then we can chill after," she replied.

"Cool," I said, leading her to LT's office.

"Nigga, your ass still ugly as fuck!" I said to LT as soon as I walked in.

"Awe, nigga, fuck you with your crispy black ass," he took a jab at me.

Sharing a laugh, we shook up.

"Well damn, who's the sexy ass queen?" he asked, staring at Kasha like she was a whole meal. Wondering how she would handle it, I let her reply.

"I can be either a beautiful dream or a beautiful nightmare, that depends on you. Yayo says you can get my shipment to me. Care to breakdown numbers, or I have to pretend to like you?" She let him know with a sexy smirk on her face. Low-key I was fist pumping like, *Der go my bitch,* but I decided to keep a straight face.

"DAMN, shawty don't play huh? Yeah, shawty I'm the man for the job. Have a seat while I breakdown this master plan for you," LT's said getting into business mode.

Thirty minutes later, the business part was done, and now I wanted to have a good time.

"You trying to fuck with the kid and let me show you how we do in Miami?" I asked Kasha with a toothless smile.

"Yeah daddy, show me how you get it!" She teased.

Ordering two bottles of Ace of Shade, we proceed to get fucking lit. After getting our bottles we went into VIP with all the stripper hoes following us.

"I'm about to get some ones, let's cut up," Kasha let me know.

All of a sudden, I heard the DJ cut the music off and I was confused.

"I don't know who shawty is that just ordered ten thousand for VIP but shit about to get popping in this bitch!" I heard DJ Major Boi say over the microphone.

Shaking my head, I knew it was Kasha's ass. Stepping back into the booth, she sat on my lap.

"I'm going to take over your city, lil nigga," she said as the bottle girl came with the single dollar bills.

"Nah baby girl, you don't have to do that, the city is mine. Since you're going to be mine also it's yours too," I said as I bit down on my bottom lip.

By this time, all the dancers were in our section. Kasha stood up grabbing a bundle of ones. She went to the balcony and threw them in the crowd, making a money shower. I cackled a little because some of the dancers went running back into the crowd to pick them up. Taking her seat back on my lap, she began dancing as Hood Celebrity's *Walking Trophy,* boomed through the club.

Kasha twerked her ass on me to the music. My eyes were following her as her body moved calculatingly. She was in her zone grinding until she placed her hand over her bullet wound. Wincing in pain, she sat down, and our eyes connected.

"You ok?" I damn near yelped.

"I'm fine, I'll take my medicine when we get back. Until then, can you be that for me?" she cooed.

"What, your medicine?"

She smirked and shook her head seductively. Damn, shawty was fucking up my head already.

March releases!

39108553R00175

Made in the USA
Middletown, DE
14 March 2019